Rainbow Beauty

Peppermint Kiss

Kelly McKain

USBORNE

First published in 2013 by Usborne Publishing Ltd., Usborne House,
83-85 Saffron Hill, London EC1N 8RT, England.
www.usborne.com

Illustration copyright © Usborne Publishing Ltd., 2013
Illustrations by Antonia Miller.

A CIP catalogue record for this book is available from the British Library.

JFMAMJJASON /12   02806/1   ISBN 9781409539605
Printed in Reading, Berkshire, UK.

Chapter One

"So, like, where's the rest of it?"

Sapphire opened a door off the kitchen, looking for more rooms, or perhaps stairs to another floor, and found a cupboard with a high window instead. Inside was an ancient vacuum cleaner, which, judging by the state of the flat, hadn't been used for at least fifteen years.

"I know it's compact—" Mum began, but Grace, who was peering round another doorway, cut in: "There are beds in the sitting room. How weird."

"Well, we'll probably have to do without a lounge for now," Mum muttered. "I thought you and Saff could have that room—"

My two older sisters stared at each other, then at Mum, in horror. "What — share?!" they both cried at once.

"But I can't have all her clothes and shoes and stuff in MY room! You know how messy she is!" (That was Grace.)

"I can't relax with her in MY room, wanting to study all the time. I can't creep around in silence, I need to express myself!" (Saff that time.)

"What about Abbie?" Grace said then. "It's not fair she's getting her own room — I'm the one with GCSEs next year!"

I looked at Mum. "Yeah, what *about* me?" I asked. I didn't think I'd seen a third bedroom, and it would have been hard to miss in a place this small.

Mum gave me a strained smile. "Well, I thought *we* could—"

Not joking, my mouth actually dropped open. "No way!" I gasped. "I'm nearly fourteen, not four! I can't share a room with my MUM! I'd rather sleep in that cupboard!"

"Okay, I'll go in with Saff," Grace said quickly.

"No way!" Saff cried. "I'd rather have Abbie."

My gaze skipped across all three of them, trying to work out who would be the least hideous option. But I couldn't think straight. Grace and Saff were shouting at each other by then, and at Mum, and she was shouting back, telling them to calm down…and then I saw it. It just ran across the hall in front of me. "RAT!" I screeched.

We all absolutely screamed our heads off, and jumped up on the peeling plastic chairs.

"Oh my gosh, where's it gone?" Mum shrieked.

"It ran down the hall!" I cried.

"Someone get a broom!" yelled Saff.

"I am NOT leaving this chair!" Mum squealed.

"Don't be ridiculous, it's only a rat," Grace snapped. "Behaving like this is what gives women a bad name."

Just then there was a flash of fur and tail as the rat ran back across the doorway. We all screamed again, and Grace clambered onto the wobbly sticky-topped kitchen table. Then…

"Dad! Help!" I yelled.

Honestly, it just came flying out of my mouth on its own. We were all plunged into shocked silence. You could feel the pain, buzzing and pulsing between us like electricity. Snapping and sparking and sizzling. I glanced quickly at Mum, hoping I hadn't made her cry. But she just looked ragged and defeated and numb, which was worse somehow.

I suppose I should say what happened, why Dad's

not here. I mean, even though I don't really want to talk about it. Okay, so, deep breath…

Mum and Dad have split up. Dad had an affair, Mum found out, and our whole world just seemed to explode. He ended it straight away, but that didn't seem to make things any better. At first they tried to talk about it – in fact we *all* did once, sitting down together round our big chunky kitchen table (Mum's idea). Yes, it *was* the most embarrassing half hour of my life, in case you're wondering. But the talking didn't work – instead it always seemed to turn into shouting, then crying, then door-slamming and silence.

And then we woke up that morning three weeks ago to find Dad gone. Well, I did. Grace and Saff were still in bed. So was Mum, I saw, as I crept across her and Dad's room to nab some of her re-shine hair serum. As soon as I walked into their en suite, I knew something was wrong, although it took me a while to work out what.

7.30 a.m. It should have still smelled of shaving soap, but the shaving soap wasn't even *there*, or the razor, or the strip of disposable contact lenses and the pair of cufflinks that sat beside them. I felt a sudden knot in my stomach. I sneaked out again and tiptoed down the stairs, my heart pounding.

Dad should have been making fresh coffee from the built-in Italian machine, grinding beans and frothing milk in the special little jug. But there was no coffee smell. No hiss and bubble of the milk steamer. No Dad.

I'd stared at our kitchen table, the place where we'd had so many fun Friday takeaway nights and lazed about on Sunday mornings, peeling vegetables or painting our nails. There was always chatter, with everyone coming and going, sitting down for a quick cuppa and a flick through a mag, or spreading out homework for long afternoons. That table had been covered with birthday cakes and Christmas turkeys, and sometimes late-night tears and hot chocolate, when Sapphire's latest crush had turned into yet another disaster, or when Grace had got less than top marks on some test or other.

Now it was empty, except for a note in Dad's scribbly handwriting, on the back of an envelope. One word.

Sorry.

"Sorry," I murmured then, looking anxiously at Mum again. That seemed to bring us all out of our trance.

Her eyes filled with tears as she leaned across and hugged me. "There is *nothing* for you to be sorry about," she said, her voice going as wobbly as the chair I was standing on.

"I'll make some tea," Grace mumbled, as we climbed down.

Just then, a knock at the door made us all jump. We were on the first floor, the only flat up this stairway, and the shop unit below was empty. "That'll be the landlord," said Mum. "Mr. Vulmer."

"Perfect timing," Saff said haughtily. "Now you can tell him it's all been a horrible mistake and that we're leaving – pronto."

"Shush!" Mum hissed.

We stood in the kitchen doorway and had a quick row over who was going to walk past the "rat bit" to get to the front door, and finally Mum went, springing across the carpet on tiptoes to touch it as little as possible, even though she had her shoes on.

She smoothed down her hair and adjusted her jumper and skirt before opening the door, as she always did. There stood Mr. Vulmer, wheezing from the effort of climbing one flight of stairs, his huge belly spilling out from under a polyester top that released this horrible smell of sweat, stale bacon fat and cigarettes. I actually had to stop myself from wrinkling up my nose, and I tried to smile politely as he waddled past us into the kitchen. We all looked at

Mum, waiting for her to break the news that we were leaving.

But instead she started chatting on pretend-brightly about how convenient it was to be near the shops (we were right above a parade of them – not that I'd call the wool shop, chippy and laundrette I'd seen exactly *useful*). Then she offered him a cup of tea. But he just snorted, like something was funny. "No thanks, Mrs. Green," he wheezed. "I'm not the welcoming committee. I've just come for my money. A month's rent and the same as a deposit, as we agreed on the phone."

Mum turned around, kettle in hand, looking astonished. "What – now?" she stuttered.

Mr. Vulmer frowned. "Yeah. You're here, aren't you?"

"Yes, but, well…I hadn't realized. I thought… there are still contracts to be signed, and I was going to organize the direct debit tomorrow, when the bank's open, and…" She pulled herself up, looked him in the eye and added bravely, "Also, there are a few things we're not happy with. We've just seen a *rat*. And the mattresses are in a terrible state. We'll need these things remedied before I'm willing to pay the full amount."

Mr. Vulmer let out a wheezy laugh, which ended

in a minor choking fit. "You're not from round here, are you, love?" he spluttered. "I don't *do* direct debit."

Mum looked helpless, but Saff had had enough by then. "It's irrelevant, because we're not staying in this dive anyway," she said snottily.

Mr. Vulmer wasn't laughing then.

"She just means that unfortunately there's been a mistake," said Grace, cutting in quickly to smooth things over. "Regrettably, this flat isn't suitable for our needs. Tomorrow morning we'll go straight into town and find something more...*appropriate*."

Saff looked horrified. "Tomorrow morning?" she squealed. "You're having a laugh! I'm not staying one second longer!" She turned to Mr. Vulmer and flicked her long chestnut hair imperiously. "We'll book into that spa hotel I saw on the edge of town for tonight. If you could just help us with our suitcases—"

Mr. Vulmer stared at her, his eyes bulging slightly. We all held our breath – we didn't know if he was going to do his wheezy laugh again or shout in her face. It was the laugh luckily – he probably didn't have enough breath for shouting. But his voice had a nasty edge all the same. "Well, I'm sorry the accommodation isn't up to Madame's standards. Fine, go then – I'm well shot of you. But be warned

12

– if you're still here tomorrow, I'll want at least a week's rent on the spot, otherwise you'll be out on the street."

He lurched back up the hallway, squeezing past our stacked pile of stuff, and opened the door. He lumbered through, turned and said, "Oh and there's a box of rat poison under the sink. That usually does the trick." Then he slammed the door behind him.

"Urgh!" cried Saff, shuddering dramatically. "What a horrible man! Anyway, let's get going. I think that nice hotel was called the Royal Devon or something. I'll ring for a cab to take us there." She pulled out her slim pink mobile and stabbed in 118 118 with a perfectly-manicured purple fingernail.

"There's no money," Mum mumbled.

"That's okay," said Grace, "I can pay for the taxi with my last bit of cash and then what money do we need? Everything else can go on your Amex."

"Too right – let Dad pick up the tab," Saff grumbled. Then she frowned at her phone. "Hey, that's weird, I'm not getting through – there's just this *beeeep*." She held it up to the ceiling and waved it around. "Typical if there's no signal in this hellhole."

"Abs, if it's a spa hotel it's bound to have a pool,

so when we get there we can go for a swim if you like," said Grace. "I forgot my cozzie but these sort of places always have a little shop. We can get new ones."

That cheered me up a lot. I love swimming. It's one of the things Mum promised we'd be able to do more of if we came down here.

The move had only been decided after school the day before. Mum had said it would just be for a few weeks, a couple of months at the most, to get some country air and clear our heads. Saff had finished her GCSEs a couple of weeks earlier and there was only a month of the summer term left for me and Grace. Mum doesn't usually let us have a day off unless we're on death's doorstep, but she said she'd found this fab summer school down here that we could go to for a few weeks, with art and cookery and crafts for me, and a top maths tutor for Grace. And amazing grounds with a swimming pool. She'd made it sound like just the change of scene we needed.

We hadn't had time to say goodbye to our friends – I'd texted Em and Zo on the way down, letting them know I wouldn't be back till September, and inviting them to stay sometime. But no way was I bringing them *here*. Mum had come down to Devon on a yoga retreat last year, and she'd made Totnes sound like an amazing, magical place. Well, there was nothing amazing or magical about it so far.

Suddenly I felt really uneasy. "What are we doing here, Mum?" I asked. "In this flat, I mean. It *is* just a mistake, isn't it?"

Mum sighed. Then she said, "I'm so sorry, girls, it's not a mistake. There's *no* money. As in, no Amex. No credit cards at all. And Saff, it's not the signal. Your phone's been cut off."

"WHAT?! How DARE he do this to us!" Saff shrieked, obviously meaning Dad. "How could he be so spiteful? He's the one in the wrong!" She glared at Mum. "Right, well done for trying to be independent and everything, but I'm taking charge here — someone's got to. I'm ringing Dad this minute to come and take us home — it's his duty, this is his mess after all. And it's totally out of order that he's cut off our money. I'm not having it, I'm just not."

Grace tutted loudly. "I'm not going anywhere with *him*. The money situation will have to be sorted out — it's his duty to support us. And he can at least pay our deposit for another flat until things are sorted out officially. I suppose we'll have to camp out here tonight after all and then get down to the letting agents' first thing in the morning."

"With no job?" Mum asked wearily. "With no

references and no income? No one will even consider renting me anywhere. I had to go with this place, it was our only choice. And I haven't even got the money for *this*. I didn't realize he'd want it up front."

We all looked at her in total horror. My stomach felt like a dishcloth being wrung out as I started to realize what a mess we were in.

"But *Dad* can just pay it for us, can't he?" asked Grace, looking uneasy.

"I don't get why we didn't just stay in our house in Ealing if this is what we were coming to," said Saff.

That's what *I* was wondering – Dad had gone, after all. He was the one who'd had the affair. The wife and kids got the house, didn't they? It was the way things were.

That's when Mum started crying, big choking sobs from deep inside. We weren't expecting that. My sisters looked as worried as I felt. "It's okay, we'll sort it," said Saff more gently, as we led Mum to the revolting brown sofa shoved in the corner of the kitchen and sat her down.

"Please don't cry," Grace begged.

Mum finally got enough breath back to speak, her words coming out in sharp, tear-choked bursts. "I was only trying to protect you. I couldn't face telling you the truth. The house… It's gone. Repossessed by the bank."

"What?" shrieked Saff.

"Oh my gosh," murmured Grace.

My head felt numb. Like the words wouldn't go in.

In a torrent, Mum poured out the whole story. We'd known about the affair, but it turned out that Dad had been keeping a whole load of other secrets from us too. His business had been struggling and he'd run up massive debts. Just the day before, he'd called Mum and finally told her how bad it really was – that the bank would be repossessing the house and debt collectors were on their way to take anything they could to make up for the money he owed. If we hadn't left when we did, right at that moment, we'd have lost all our personal things too.

"So there actually isn't *any* money?" Saff gasped.

Suddenly I felt really, really angry, like I'd been tricked. "What about the summer school?" I demanded. "And Grace's tutor? Saff's new car and driving lessons… Was it all lies? All of it?"

Saff put her arm round me and glared at Mum.

"I'm so sorry, girls," Mum stuttered. "I shouldn't have lied. It was all such a shock – I just panicked. I knew we were running out of time, so I just said whatever I could think of to make you pack your stuff and come with me." She sighed heavily. "I really am sorry," she said again.

"Well, that's ruined my chances of getting into Cambridge then, hasn't it?" Grace snapped. "Thanks very much!"

"So you're saying this is it? This flat?" I stammered. "This is our life now?"

Saff just looked bewildered. "Has all our stuff been taken?" she murmured.

Mum's face crumpled again. "I hope not. Roger and Laura next door offered to move as many of our belongings as they could into their garage, but I don't know how far they got before the debt people turned up."

"How dare those men just walk into our house! We should have locked ourselves in and called the police!" Grace cried.

Mum shrugged. "It's not our house any more."

I imagined two scary men with bomber jackets and shaved heads riffling through our cupboards and drawers, pulling out our ballet shoes and board games, tennis racquets, ski suits, recipe books, the pottery animals we'd made in primary school. It made me feel really sick.

"But why didn't Dad just tell us the truth when

things started to go wrong?" Grace asked. "It might not have got so bad then."

Mum found a tissue in her bag and blew her nose. "I think he'd been living in a fantasy world, acting like everything was great, spending *more* than usual, and having an affair. Desperately running away from the facts, basically."

All I could think about was that yesterday, while Dad had been telling Mum what was about to happen to us, I'd been in double Science, worrying about why my litmus paper wasn't going pink like Em and Zo's, and giggling with them about how geeky we looked in our safety goggles. I'd had no idea that my whole world was about to change. Again.

Mum sighed. "So now your dad's moved into some horrible bedsit, and he's going to declare bankruptcy. He can't give us anything because he's got nothing to give."

We were all silent, in utter shock. How could Dad have let this *happen* to us? Then, as I was still staring numbly at the peeling kitchen worktop, Grace and Saff went into meltdown.

"Oh my gosh, we really are stuck here, aren't we?" cried Grace, panic in her voice.

"What about my friends? And my singing lessons?" screeched Saff. "You know I've already

19

enrolled for Arts Ed in September! How could you do this to me?"

They both stared at Mum as if she'd taken their dreams, thrown them on the floor and stomped them to smithereens.

As for me, of course I was scared. Terrified. I mean, I'd just found out that I'd lost my home, my friends, my *life*, and that we had no money (how would we even buy food?). And everything I owned now fitted into a suitcase. But as for my *dream*, well, that had already been ruined. I'd only ever wanted one thing: a big, cosy, rowdy, happy family – me, Mum, Dad, Saff and Grace all together. And that had gone when we found out about the affair. To me, the fact that we were now penniless and stuck in a disgusting flat, with a repulsive landlord and at least one rat… Well, that was just the rancid icing on the mouldy cake. "None of this is Mum's fault," I told my sisters firmly. "What else could she do? Seriously – what?"

Thankfully that made them stop freaking out for long enough for Mum to speak. "Please, girls, I'm begging you to give this a go," she gabbled. "I suppose we could have gone running to Granny and Grandpa, but they don't have enough room for us all, and anyway, I really, *really* want us to do this on our own."

Wow, if Mum thought the only other option was moving us to Yorkshire to live with Granny she really must have been desperate. They don't exactly get on.

"I'm going to look for work first thing in the morning," she said then. "Thank goodness I managed to finish my yoga teacher training before…all this. There are plenty of places I can give classes around here. Grace and Abbie, I've spoken to the education department at Devon County Council and they've been able to make emergency arrangements for us. You're enrolled in the local school, to start tomorrow."

We both gasped. *Tomorrow?*

"No way, I——" Grace began.

But: "Please, just give it a go, that's all I'm asking," Mum begged. "Go for one day, and if you hate it we'll have a rethink."

Grace sighed, but she didn't say anything else.

Mum turned to Saff. "I thought you could go down to the college in Paignton and see what beauty courses there are to start in September," she said, almost in a whisper. "You've always been interested in that kind of thing."

"Yeah, as in I like being pampered," Saff spat. "I'm not going to be some boring old beauty therapist like you were. Forget it. I'm going to *be* someone!"

The way Mum flinched, Saff may as well have slapped her. She used to be a beautician before she married Dad and had us three. She did sometimes talk about going back to work, but then a few years ago, when Dad's corporate events business took off, we moved to the big house in Ealing, and they got the matching Range Rovers. After that, Mum was only ever the one *getting* beauty treatments, not giving them.

I gave Saff a sharp nudge in the ribs. "Ow! Jeez, Abs!" she complained. But then she sighed and said, "I'm sorry, Mum, I didn't mean it like that. This is just such a lot to take in. Look, let's all try to get some sleep tonight – we can put towels in the gaps under our doors so the *thing* can't get us. And I'll go down the college tomorrow, just to look."

"I'll give the school a go for one day, if you will," I said to Grace.

She grimaced, but muttered, "Deal."

Mum smiled weakly, although tears were now sliding down her cheeks again. "Thanks," she said, her voice cracking. "Oh, come here, my girls, my lovely girls."

We all snuggled together on the vile sofa, our feet tucked up behind us in case the rat decided to make another run for it. We watched the last of the light fade outside the kitchen window, and we didn't move until long after dark.

Chapter Two

As you can guess, we didn't get much sleep. The double bed creaked and groaned every time Mum turned over (which was about every five minutes *all night*) and it took me ages to find a position that didn't let any of the horrible spiny broken spring bits dig into me.

I woke up to the sound of Saff banging around in the kitchen — it was only half seven, way too early for her to be up usually, but she said the curtains were so thin the light had woken her. Not that it was bright sunshine outside or anything — instead the sky just looked a menacing, moody grey, like there was a storm brewing.

Grace staggered in, wearing wellies with her nightie (she'd gone and got them out of the boot of the car), and armed with the broom, in case the rat reappeared. Mum wandered in too and put the kettle on, and soon the four of us were sitting round the table sipping Price Cutter tea in bleary-eyed silence. For the first time ever, no one made a dash to hog the bathroom.

I had a quick shower using the attachment over the bath, while trying not to let the manky plastic curtain stick to my legs. Thank goodness I'd bought all my yummy home-made bath stuff with me. Of course, being me, it was the first thing I'd grabbed when Mum said we were going, especially as she'd told me there would be soap-making in the craft lessons at summer school. In fact, once I'd packed all my home-made products, plus the flower petals and rosebuds, soap and bath foam bases, essential oils, moulds, ribbons, bottles, jars, vintage compacts and sparkly pens I used to make them, it hadn't left room for much more than a couple of pairs of jeans, and a few tops and skirts in my suitcase.

I wanted to wear my own clothes to the new school, but Mum rummaged in one of her suitcases and produced my uniform (even though it probably wasn't the right colour – pea-green, anyone?), including the regulation nun-thickness tights and flat brown loafers. I was going to argue, but she looked so exhausted I just put the whole lot on, even the tights (sorry, but no way was I showing my milk-white legs, not even in June – the glare from them might dazzle a driver and cause an accident). But at least I smelled nice, thanks to my zingy lemon shower gel and rose moisturizer.

Luckily, I'd remembered to grab my make-up bag too. I spent ages in front of the cracked bathroom mirror, making my eyes look really big with layers of silver and grey eyeshadow, a dark-blue eye pencil and about seven coats of black mascara. I'm one of those people who *need* make-up to bring their face to life – otherwise, with my long light-blonde hair, pale skin and barely-there eyebrows, it hardly looks like I have a head. I finished off with a slick of nude lip gloss and bushed my hair up a bit before gathering it into a low side bunch, making sure a few strands were sticking out so it looked as messed-up as possible.

We all left the flat together and of course automatically headed for the Range Rover. Saff said spikily that it was a miracle it was still there, in this kind of neighbourhood, and Mum replied pointedly that it wouldn't be for long, not once the bailiffs tracked us down. She wanted to conserve the little bit of petrol we had in case there was an emergency though, so we had to walk. Halfway into town, Saff peeled off onto the road where the bus stop for Paignton was. Mum had wanted to go with her, but Saff had pointed out that finding work was the priority for her. I linked arms with Grace and did a little hop so that we were in step, our matching foul loafers stomping along the pavement together. They looked even worse next to Mum's gorgeous Italian heels.

We reached the gate of Cavendish High and found that the playground was empty and silent. For one happy moment I thought the school must be shut and that we wouldn't have to go, but when a car pulled up and a girl got out and hurried past us, I realized that we were late. "Oh gosh, I must have got the time wrong," Mum muttered. "I'm sorry, girls, I've just had so much on my mind…"

I forced myself to smile and insisted it didn't matter, but inside it made me feel even more nervous. I tried to step through the gate, but Grace leaped backwards, as if there was an invisible force field across the entrance. I had to grip her arm hard for a moment, because I thought she was going to bolt off down the road.

"Come on, Gracie, you can do this," Mum said. Grace looked uncertainly at her, but fat drops of rain had started plopping onto us, and that seemed to make up her mind. "Fine," she grumbled, "but only for one day. That's all we promised."

We trooped in through the main doors and Mum smoothed down her jacket and skirt before ushering us into the school office. The secretary smiled and welcomed us and sat Mum down with a pile of forms to fill in. "You've missed registration, and you're late for first lesson, I'm afraid," she told Grace and me, frowning at the timetable in her hands. "I'll take you over to 10D, Grace. They're in the science block and it's quite a walk from here. Abbie, you can hurry off to join 9L, they're only just down in Humanities. Mr. Carver's expecting you. It's left after the double doors there, follow the corridor, out across the courtyard and first door on the right. Okay, dear?"

"Shall I come with you?" asked Mum, looking anxious.

I pulled on my fake smile again. "I'll be fine," I told her, when actually I hadn't taken in a word that the secretary had said. Besides, Mum's lovely, and actually pretty cool, but still, I think walking into class with my *mum* in tow would have been a bit of a first-day blunder. I hugged her goodbye, then Grace,

28

took a deep breath and hurried off along the corridor.

The rain was splashing down harder as I headed out of the double doors. It didn't look like a courtyard exactly, and I couldn't see a door, but maybe the secretary had said to follow the path round to the right to find it? As I hurried along beside some bins (still no door to be seen) there was a rumble of thunder and the storm broke.

Then it absolutely poured down.

I tried to run back round to the doors I'd come out of, but I must have taken a wrong turn and I ended up by a totally different building, like a gym hall or something. My jumper was completely soaked through and dripping, and the sleeves were getting longer and longer, so I pulled it off over my head as I ran. Rain was pouring down my face and into my eyes, so I could hardly see where I was going, and I was so totally lost and confused by then, I didn't know which direction to run in anyway. The sky flashed with lightning, and then boomed with thunder a second later. I squealed and stood rigid, stuck to the spot, panicking.

"Hey! In here!"

I whirled round, trying to find where the voice was coming from. A boy was waving at me from a narrow doorway. I ran towards him, each step squelching, and as I got close he dashed out and bundled me in. I clung onto him for a moment, without thinking, like you would if someone really had just rescued you from drowning. Then I realized I was hugging a complete stranger and pulled away.

And then I looked at him.

And I mean, well. OMG. I just could not *stop* looking at him. His piercing blue eyes. His rain-slicked black hair. His olive skin and wide smile.

The lightning struck again.

He took off his blazer and as he put it round my shoulders I got a big shiver – nothing to do with being cold. I smiled thanks and shrugged it on, breathing in its lovely smell, picking up cinnamon and musk. As the silence grew, I fumbled for something to say. I opened my mouth but found that no words would come out while I was still staring at him, so I dragged my eyes away, out to the storm raging around us. "Yuck, it's really pouring now." Oh dear. *Abbie Green, stater of the obvious.*

I just *had* to look at him again and I saw that he was grinning gorgeously. "Without the rain, you wouldn't have rainbows," he said.

That made me snort with laughter (yikes – how attractive!). "True," I said, "if cheesy. I'm Abbie." I held out my hand. Goodness knows why, it looked

30

like I thought I was at a business meeting or something, and it seemed especially stupid after the, you know, *hugging*.

He raised an eyebrow and shook my hand. "Marco."

I felt a little jump of electricity between us, and I had to actually *force* myself to let go. Seriously, I pretty much needed to use my other hand to prise my fingers off him.

"Late?" he asked.

I nodded.

"Me too," he said. "Where are you headed? You must be new. I haven't seen you around before and, believe me, I would have noticed."

My stomach flipped over. I tried to think of something sparkling and flirty to say back, but all I managed was, "I'm meant to be in 9L."

He grinned. "That's my form. It must be fate. The rain's easing off now, let's go for it." My stomach did a double flip as he took my hand, pulling me along. Together we ran round a corner and into a doorway – so I wasn't that far off after all.

I wiped my feet on the mat thing, caught sight of myself in the glass door and immediately died of embarrassment. I looked like a cross between a drowned rat and a glam rocker, with my hair plastered flat to my head and make-up running all down my face in little black rivers.

Oh *bleeping bleep*! I just had to get away from this Marco person and into the loos to fix my make-up meltdown as soon as possible, before *this* image of me got imprinted onto his brain for ever. I pulled off his blazer. "Here, thanks for this," I said, trying to hand it back. I glanced down and realized the nun-thickness tights had stretched in the rain and were now bunched in soggy pools round my ankles. Just to complete the look.

"No. Keep it for today, it's fine," he muttered.

"No, here, I'll be okay now," I insisted, waving it at him, still looking down at my tragic tights.

"No, really, hang on to it," he said again.

I looked up at last. "Honestly, I'm fine, just take—" I stopped talking as I watched his gaze slide quickly from my face to my chest and back to my face again, while he did a strange feet-shuffling, throat-clearing thing.

At this point you're thinking it couldn't have got any worse, right? But it had. I glanced down too and absolutely *spun* in my grave of embarrassment. My shirt had gone see-through and (oh no! Oh *yes*!) my entire *bra* was showing. I clapped the blazer to my chest, then pulled it back on, writhing around like a snake to keep everything covered up while I was getting my arms in. Like a true gentleman, Marco was staring in completely the other direction, looking extremely interested in a wall display about how to make biodiesel from chip fat.

Thank goodness a teacher came by then and hurried us off to class, or we might have been stuck there, too embarrassed to move or say anything until, like, *the end of time*. And luckily it was impossible for me to BE more embarrassed by then, because now I had to make my new-school debut with a dripping-wet spam head and scary clown make-up, in my stupidly prissy, posh pea-green gear with the nun-tights flapping round my ankles.

My stomach lurched with nerves as I followed Marco into the classroom and stared around me. Really, I would have fitted in better by wearing my own stuff, because everyone else was in only the tiniest *hint* of uniform. The surf-dude types wore theirs with zip-up tops and beanie hats, the Emos with bandana scarves and black skinny jeans, and the townies with gold chains, crop tops and velour trackies (just the girl ones, obviously. They also had so much foundation on I thought it might crack and drop off when a couple of them smirked at the state of me).

Whatever group they were in, everyone gave me the same look, like I'd just landed from outer space. I turned to the teacher, thinking he'd introduce me, or even (please, please) let me go and dry off in the loos. But instead he just gave me a moody glare and said, "Abigail Green, I assume. Take a seat, quickly. You've disrupted this class enough already."

Luckily, Marco ushered me over to his table. I squelched across the room and took the spare chair, and the teacher started talking again (I've no idea what about). The brown-haired boy sitting opposite me (with his shirt unbuttoned to display a Scooby Doo T-shirt underneath) gave me a warm smile and I smiled back. You know how it is with some people. You just get a good vibe.

When I glanced over to the girl next to me, she smiled too. "I'm Summer," she whispered. "That's Ben. And I gather you've met Mr. Vain." She winked at Marco and sang, "Yeah-yeah, I wanna be a rock star," under her breath. He grinned and flicked her a V-sign.

Out of everyone in the room, Summer had taken her uniform closest to the limit with hippy bracelets and beads, stripy tights, DMs with painted flowers on, a minuscule skirt and a huge floppy yellow bow in her long curly black hair. She looked A. Mazing.

Snuggling up in Marco's blazer, and enjoying the

smell of his body spray or whatever it was swirling all around me (I was picking up the cedar wood from it now as well), I felt like things might not be going too badly after all.

At break, Summer showed me where the loos were and I got a chance to dry off my hair and shirt under the hand dryer. The nun tights were still soggy and stretching evilly. At this rate they were only ever going to fit someone eight foot tall, so I took them off and threw them in the bin. My make-up was so wrecked the only choice I had was to scrub it all off. Which meant I'd be stuck like that for the rest of the day – bare-faced. Yikes. Kids were probably going to be staring at me in the corridor, asking each other, "Where *has* that girl's head gone?"

How on earth could I forget to bring any make-up to school? How could Summer not have any with her? I did get why not, actually. Some girls don't need it. Summer looked amazing with just a slick of Lypsyl – her eyelashes were naturally full and dark, her skin was peachy and her cheeks were slightly flushed in a gorgeous way you could never achieve with a blusher brush. Grrr. I'm not saying I wished she could be ugly for *ever* or anything, but maybe just for the day, because standing next to her was making me look even *worse*.

"I'll bring you some uniform stuff I've grown out of," she offered, and I just automatically said, "Oh thanks, that's really sweet, but I'll buy it new."

She peered at me. "Oh, okay." She looked a bit shocked. "It's just better to reuse stuff, isn't it?" she said then. "You know, reduce, reuse, recycle and all that."

Huh. I mean, obviously we put our bottles and cans out for the recycling truck like everyone else, but I'd never thought having second-hand uniform could be seen as a *good* thing. New was just better… wasn't it?

Lots of things were different here though.

Like, at my old school we all did our ties in a certain way, with only the thin bit hanging down. We thought it made us look so individual. But now I realized it just made us all look the same. The kids here who even had ties *on* were wearing them in so many different ways – short, fat knot, skinny, loose, even just the regular way. Anyone who'd turned up like that at my old school would have been teased so badly, it wasn't worth it…but here no one seemed to care.

So then I said yes please to Summer's offer of uniform, pretending it was only because I wanted to be green, and not also because – as I'd remembered – we couldn't actually afford anything new.

36

When I'd finished making myself look even *less* attractive in the loos, we went into the dining hall. The canteen was open for snacks and I realized all at once that, a), I was starving hungry and, b), I'd forgotten to bring any money with me. Then I remembered that I didn't have any money *to* bring, and that was such a weird feeling. Dad was always slipping us tenners, he paid for our phones by direct debit, and I had a monthly allowance for supplies for making my soaps and stuff, plus any clothes or downloads I wanted. *Used* to have, I realized with a start.

Summer pulled an apple out of her bag and crunched into it. I followed her to a table and we sat down. "Don't you want anything?" she asked, gesturing towards the counter, where the boys were queuing.

"Oh, I'm fine, thanks," I said breezily, hoping my stomach wouldn't rumble. "I had a massive breakfast."

Actually, I'd been too nervous to eat anything that morning, and I'd forgotten to bring the sandwiches Mum had made me (the Price Cutter white bread, marg and cheap cheese spread hadn't looked exactly *appealing*, but I'd happily have wolfed them down now). Thank goodness I'd filled up an old water bottle I had in my bag, so I could glug that at least.

Marco and Ben came over then, each stuffing down an iced bun as they walked. My stomach lurched with envy. But then Ben put a plate down in front of me with a white-iced one on, and grinned. "Got you this."

I felt flustered. "Thanks, but…I'll have to owe you. I—" In panic, I reached for something to say. "I forgot my purse."

He beamed again and said through a mouthful of iced bun, "On me. Welcome present."

I thanked him and tucked in. See? Told you. Good vibe.

We all chatted a bit (I didn't say much about me – I didn't feel ready to go there yet). Mostly, they filled me in on the school. They reckoned I'd had bad luck that morning, getting Mr. Carver first off. He was the strictest teacher in the entire school, apparently.

They also told me about a Media Diploma option that was all design and film-making and photography and that kind of thing. They'd started it that year and you could do it right up to Year 11 and it counted as five GCSEs in the end. I'm really interested in all that kind of stuff, so I planned to put myself down for it at my lunchtime meeting with my form teacher, Mrs. Lurman. "I'm going to ask her about joining the lacrosse team too," I said. "And the swimming club. How long's your pool?"

"Erm, we don't do lacrosse," said Summer. "And there's no pool here."

"Oh," I said, blushing enough to power the whole of Totnes.

"You can take the girl out of posh school, but you can't take posh school out of the girl!" Marco joked, making me blush even more, probably enough to power most of Devon.

Summer shot him a killer look, then turned to me. "There's one at The Pavilion in town though," she said. "That's the leisure centre."

"The school swimming club meets there every week," Ben added. "My mate Zak goes. He says it's a laugh."

"And there's hockey in winter and netball at the moment," said Summer.

"Oh, that's good," I mumbled. "I like netball too."

While we were talking I tried really hard to act normal around Marco. But once or twice I found myself staring at him like some kind of crazy stalker. I had to tear my eyes away and make myself look at

Summer and Ben too, and other places people usually look when they haven't been struck down by a *massive bone-shaking crush*, like at the table and round the room.

"Are you up for coming to Marco's next gig?" Summer asked.

"Oh, are you in a band then?" I found myself asking him. Duh. Stupid question.

"Yeah, Headrush," he said, as I tried to look at him in a normal, how-interesting-tell-me-more way and not an intense, staring, you-are-the-most-gorgeous-boy-I've-ever-seen way. "It's me and some guys from Year 10," he added. "I play lead guitar. We're kind of like The Clash, with a bit of Get Cape. Wear Cape. Fly thrown in."

Summer snorted. "You *wish!*" Then she turned to me. "It's in a couple of weeks. It's a sort of showcase for the Saturday Music Club we have here. My dad's driving me and Ben up there, so we can get you on the way if you live in town."

"Yeah, I do, well, more on the edge," I muttered, thinking that I'd have to go and stand on the corner of the street to wait for Summer's dad – no way was I letting any of them see the manky flat. That's if we were still *here* in two weeks. It was great to be invited though – and on my first day, too. And if Marco was going to be onstage, well, that was a *licence* to stare at him, wasn't it? "Is it far away then?" I asked.

"It's at Dartington," said Ben. "It's this big old hall where they have films and theatre and loads of eco stuff going on. It's really cool, you'll like it."

"We'll have to put up with his racket, unfortunately," Summer said, "but some of the other bands are okay. You can always listen to your iPod while he's playing, that's what I do."

"Charming!" Marco cried, jabbing her in the ribs. "You're being a right cow today, by the way, even more than usual."

"The cheek!" screeched Summer. "You can buy me a drink for that!" She slapped him one and they had a bit of a wrestly muck-about, which gave me a horrible lurching feeling in my stomach. Had I got this wrong? Were they more than just friends?

Were they together?

It's not like they had their arms round each other or anything obvious, but...all the mucking about, and then, at the counter, reaching for their drinks, they just seemed so close and connected...

If Marco was Summer's boyfriend that put him seriously off limits.

I just *had* to know.

Ben was saying something I didn't quite catch,

about a wildlife sanctuary, I think, when I smiled and cut in, trying to sound casual. "So, those two, are they going out?"

He actually *laughed* at that. "Yeah, as *if*. They've been mates for years, they're more like brother and sister."

I felt so relieved I had to clamp my mouth shut to stop myself from yelling, "WHOOPIEEEEEEEE!"

But then he spoiled it a bit by saying, "Marco's great and all that, but if he was going out with someone he'd have to give up his Year 8 fan club, *and* stop flirting with anything in a skirt. I don't see that happening any time soon."

That set my head spinning. He'd flirted with *me*. I'd thought it meant something but...

I desperately wanted to say to Ben, "You say he'll flirt with anything in a skirt, but just to be clear, what if the *skirt* was a repulsive pea-green one, accessorized with ever-expanding nun-thickness tights and squelchy brown loafers? Surely if someone looked like that and he still flirted with them it would *have* to mean something? Wouldn't it?"

I didn't say that, of course. I have got *some* self-respect. Okay, so probably only a tiny bit after the whole see-through-shirt episode that morning, but *some*.

"Anyway, what about you?" Ben was saying, as I came back to reality. "Seeing anyone? Course you are. Some rude boy from London. No, wait – a posh one, I bet. Crispin. *Tarquin?*"

"No one," I said distractedly, "and after the whole drowned-rat/scary-clown fandango that *everyone* saw this morning, I might as well become a nun. I've already got the tights for it. That or just wear a bag on my head for the rest of my life."

I braced myself for Ben to join in with the mickey-taking – that's why I got in there first. I mean, that's what boys do, isn't it? Put you down, for a laugh. That's what Jake and his lot from The Royal School used to do anyway, when me, Em and Zo hung out with them in Walpole Park. But Ben just smiled at me, swung his bag over his shoulder and said, "Come on, I'll show you to the science block. The early birds get the least disgusting lab coats."

Science was okay. The teacher was nicer than Mr. Carver and, apart from looking headless, I managed not to do anything to embarrass myself. Then Summer bought me lunch, luckily, because they all thought I'd forgotten my purse. I promised to pay her back, even though she insisted it was fine.

The rest of the day went okay, too. Mrs. Lurman said there was a space on the Media Diploma and gave me the website address with all the info on, so I could look at it with Mum (I needed her permission to do it). I didn't mention that we don't have a computer at the flat (and that we might not even have a *flat* after this evening). I just printed off the stuff at last break in the library instead. She also said I'd need to get some navy-coloured uniform as soon as possible, and I said, "Believe me, I'll go shopping the first chance I get, it's not as if I *enjoy* looking like this!" We both laughed a bit at that and I didn't say that we hardly had enough money for food, let alone new uniform. Thank goodness for Summer's offer.

Ben and Summer headed off as soon as the final bell went, to catch their bus, and I was left with Marco. I was just trying to think of something both hilariously funny and deeply meaningful to say, when he asked, "Fancy getting a coffee in town?"

Well, of course I did! All this stuff started running through my mind, like *Does this mean he likes me too? Or maybe he just always goes up there with whoever's around, and today it just happens to be me. Or perhaps he actually just wanted a coffee and didn't fancy sitting on his own.* I was about to say yes, but then I thought of Mum, and Saff and Grace, and suddenly I just desperately wanted to know how they were. "I'd love to, normally," I managed to mumble, "but I can't. I promised Mum I'd go straight home. First day and all that." I fumbled with the key to my locker and finally got it open. My jumper was still in a soggy heap at the bottom.

"Oh, okay, no worries. I could walk back with you," he said then.

I was just about to say, *That would be great, thanks*, but then I realized that I'd have to ask him up for a drink, and then he'd see the awful flat, and perhaps lots of rowing or crying, and possibly a RAT. He'd definitely think I was a total loser then, and I was trying to *reverse* that impression. So instead I found myself saying, "Oh, no, it's fine, thanks. My sister will be waiting for me anyway and—"

"Oh, right," he mumbled. Then when I tried to give him his blazer he just backed away, saying, "Keep it till tomorrow, or whenever, whatever." He turned and strode off down the corridor, throwing a "laterz", over his shoulder.

OMG – he gave me the "laterz" treatment. I nearly called out to him, but I stopped myself. I mean, what would I say? *Sorry, but can you not be in a mood with me because I do in fact have an agonizing, brain-numbing crush on you and I am desperate for us to go for coffee even if you don't actually mean it to mean something, but my family have been through a lot recently and I really do honestly need to get back to them.* Erm, I don't think so.

I sighed, picked up my soggy jumper and headed out. Grace was there, waiting for me at the gate. And Saff too – she'd come down from the bus stop to walk with us.

"So, how was it?" I asked them.

"Hideous!" Grace shuddered.

"Awful!" Saff wailed.

As we walked along, I found out that Grace thinks the school isn't going to challenge her enough, and Saff thinks that all the make-up and hairstyling she got to sit in on at the college looks about ten years out of date. By the time they asked me how my day went, I felt a bit guilty for actually having an okay time, so I just mumbled, "Oh, you know, alright I suppose."

We got back to the flat and found the door unlocked. As we piled into the kitchen, Grace and Saff were both already complaining loudly about their rubbish days, really gearing up for an argument with Mum about how they weren't going back. But they fell silent when we saw the state of her. She was sitting in front of a cold cup of tea, just staring into space, her eyes red from crying, looking utterly defeated.

I rushed over and put my arms around her, but she didn't hug me back.

"Mum, what's the matter?" asked Saff.

Grace just looked really anxious.

Mum smiled tensely. "Oh, I'm sorry to worry you all. Nothing awful's happened. I'm just feeling really down, that's all. I've had a horrible day. No one needs a yoga teacher – in fact, everyone round here seems to *be* one. I tried six places and everyone was really nice...but they all had more than enough staff. It was the same story with the beauty and spa places I found. So then I tried to get any job, literally anything – I asked all round town, and here in the parade. The lady in the chip shop said that a month ago they were taking on summer staff, but they've recruited everyone they need now. I guess it's the same everywhere else."

"Just as well – you don't want to work in a *chip shop*!" Saff gasped. "All that grease!"

"Surely you must be able to get an office job," Grace insisted. She adjusted her glasses and peered at Mum as if *she* was interviewing her. "You've got skills, of course—"

"Not really," said Mum. "I'm not *qualified* in anything officey. And don't be such a snob, Saff. I'd be happy to work in a chip shop, or *any* shop, or hotel or restaurant. On summer job wages I'd have to do double shifts though, what with three daughters to support. I've left my contact details with them all in case they lose someone, so hopefully I'll hear something soon. It's tough times — even very experienced people are queuing up for any vacancy that comes along."

"Well, they're welcome to it!" Saff snorted.

"I can't believe this," said Grace imperiously. "My mother is actually *hoping* to get a job as a chambermaid."

That's when I really lost it, with both of them.

"At least Mum's trying!" I snapped. "All you two have done is moan! Face it — our old life is gone. No Amex, no singing lessons, no trips to town, no posh schools, no new clothes. All that is gone. This is *it* now, got it?"

They all stared at me, stunned. Even Mum. I'd surprised myself too — hearing it out loud like that, well, I think it's the first time our situation properly began to sink into *my* head too.

"Sorry, Mum," Grace mumbled. "I didn't mean to sound...you know..."

"Nor did I," said Saff. "This has all been such a shock, that's all." She sighed. "Look, the courses on offer weren't exactly inspiring, so how about I get a job straight away instead? There's a cake factory at the edge of town that's looking for shift workers – I saw an ad on the college notice board. You can't need any special experience for that, surely? And if we asked for the same hours, we could get the bus together."

I smiled. Saff could be a nightmare sometimes, but when the chips (or chip shops!) were down, she'd do anything for our family.

I thought Mum would be pleased, too, but instead she looked furious. "Over my dead body!" she told Saff. "You are *not* missing out on your education because of what's happened. I'm just not having it. I'll find a job soon, it was only day one today. And our benefits will come through in a couple of weeks to keep us going if it takes longer. We'll manage, okay, hon? Somehow we'll survive."

Everyone was silent for what felt like ages. Then Saff said, "Well, there is a beauty course that didn't look *too* bad. And it's only four days a week, so I could work the other one, and Saturdays. I'll try to get a full-time summer job in the meantime, so I can help out with the rent straight away."

"And I'll write us a budget," Grace offered. "There are lots of things we can do to save money. Like, it'll be cheaper to walk to the big supermarket on the main road than keep going to Price Cutter for everything. And we don't need the hot water on *all* the time."

Mum smiled then, a real smile this time. "I'm so proud of you girls," she said. "I can't tell you how proud... You're right. Let's think positive. If we can just get through this month, we'll be okay."

But then came the knock at the door that made all of us go rigid.

We didn't have a month. We didn't even have a week.

Mum put her finger to her lips and we all fell silent, hardly daring to breathe.

"I know you're in there!" Mr. Vulmer shouted wheezily. "That talk about swanning off to some swanky hotel was all cobblers, wasn't it? You load of princesses, you think you're so high and mighty, don't you? Well, I'm warning you, I don't care *who* you are, no one messes me about."

Grace clung to Mum, and Saff pulled a face at the front door, but I knew she was scared too.

Weirdly I wasn't, and then with a start I realized why. Part of me was still waiting for Dad to stride over, either give Mr. Vulmer the cash or send him away empty-handed, then shut the door, cheerfully call him an idiot and ask who fancies Indian takeaway for tea. But that didn't happen, of course. And when I realized it wasn't going to, I felt scared too.

Daddy wasn't coming to rescue his princesses.

We'd have to save ourselves.

"Lucky for you lot I'm off to Malaga tomorrow," the landlord was shouting. "I'll be back this time next week though, with my keys, and if I don't get my money then, you lot'll be out on the street, and no I *won't* be carrying your (*bleep*)ing cases for you." Then we heard him blunder back down the stairs, muttering.

We all sat still and silent for ages, until we were sure he'd gone.

After getting so soaked in the morning, I was really desperate to have a bath that night, so once I'd cleaned it about a million times, I turned on the limescale-encrusted taps. Loads of steaming hot water came gushing out – that was something at least. Then I dug around in the suitcases for my special box of home-made body lotions and bath potions for some extra-special treats to cheer me up.

It's something I've always done, making my own beauty products. Mum started us off when we were little – I'd sit up on the kitchen counter, and Saff and

Grace would be on step stools alongside it. We had matching pink-striped aprons, even Mum, and we'd all be measuring and mixing and extracting and juicing and peeling and melting and stirring and setting for whole afternoons. We used so many gorgeous ingredients – like citrus peel and cinnamon sticks for bath oil, almond shells and olive grain for body scrub, blueberries and honey for fresh face masks, avocado and aloe vera for body butters. We made seaweed wraps and vanilla candles and strawberry bath bombs, packed with rose petals. We filled the house with the scents of warm spice, zingy zest and juicy berries.

Saff and Grace kind of lost interest when we moved to the Ealing house and they got their own separate hobbies and friends. Even Mum didn't do so much once she could afford to buy any products she wanted. But I've always kept up with it and, of course, they all want to borrow my things, and for me to make them stuff. Em and Zo always asked for my bath foams and solid perfumes for their birthday and Christmas presents too, and I really enjoyed coming up with the perfect blends of essential oils for them.

I took out my very favourite bath treats and lined them up on the side of the tub. Just the sight of them made me feel better, and when I poured a big slug of mandarin bath foam under the running water, the whole room filled with such a punchy burst of citrus it made my head spin.

I got in and washed with my home-made soap, breathing in its delicious jasmine and ylang-ylang smell (sometimes I use formulas from books or the net, but that's one of the recipes I made up completely by myself). Then I lay back with the last bit of my blueberry face mask on, which seemed to be okay even though it had been out of the fridge for a day. I closed my eyes and let the beautiful aromas swirl around me.

When I sat up again half an hour later and reached for my olive grain foot scrub (my poor feet needed it after spending all day in the soggy brown loafers) I felt a lot better. A week. We had a week. It wasn't long, but perhaps it would be long enough.

Chapter Three

On Thursday morning I made double-sure I had my make-up bag with me before leaving the flat. Even though it was hot and sunny, I wasn't taking any risks. Luckily, I'd persuaded Mum to just let me wear my black skirt and plain white shirt as uniform, until I could get over to Summer's and try on some of her stuff. Grace backed me up about everyone's casual gear, although she also said I looked like a waitress and that she'd stick with the pea-green look, thanks very much.

Just as Grace and I reached the school gate, a shiny motorbike came roaring up.

"Wow, cool, who's that?" I gasped. Grace tutted

and informed me that she didn't have time to stand around ogling boys (yes, she did actually use that word!). Then she hurried off to get some books from the library before the bell went.

The boy on the back of the bike got off and took off his helmet. My stomach did a full 360-degree flip when I saw it was Marco. Then it flipped right back again as the slim girl rider, who was dressed all in leathers, took off her own helmet and shook out her long dark hair, just like you see in films. Erm, next question: who was *that*?

Before I knew it, she'd stowed Marco's helmet, given him a quick hug and a kiss on the cheek, put her helmet back on and roared away. And now he was coming towards me. He looked even more gorgeous than before (if that was even possible!) in a vintage leather jacket. I tried to aim for a laid-back teasing tone, the way Summer talks to him. "So, is that your girlfriend then?" I said. "She must be at least seventeen to ride. Got yourself an older woman, have you?" Argh! It sounded more like an interrogation.

To my surprise, he looked embarrassed. "Much older," he mumbled. "That was my mum."

"Your mum?" I gasped. "OMG, did she have you when she was twelve?!"

He shrugged. "Sixteen."

"I'm so relieved it wasn't your girlfriend!" I cried before I could stop myself. ARGH! What an idiot! "Because…erm…you've got your GSCEs starting next year so you need to focus on that, and the band and everything…" I mumbled lamely.

He grinned. "Don't worry, Abs, I've only got eyes for you," he said, flinging his arm round me.

I laughed and nudged him hard, trying to act like it was just friendly mucking around. You know, as if my knees weren't about to give way at any moment.

"Is your dad into bikes too, then?" I managed to ask.

It was just for something to say, but I'd obviously hit a nerve. Marco's arm dropped to his side and the smile fell from his face. "He's not around much," he mumbled. "I mean, he is, but… Him and Mum have been on and off for years. He comes and goes. Goes, mainly."

"Oh, right," I said. He looked so awkward that I didn't push it. "My dad's not around either," I said then, surprising myself.

"Oh," said Marco. The bell went and we began to wander in. "What happened?" he asked.

"You know, the usual," I said, trying to sound offhand about it. "He had an affair, Mum found out, they split up, his business failed and we got kicked out of our house. That's why we moved here."

Marco stopped still, staring at me. He looked shocked. I was a bit shocked too, actually. Had I really just said that? "Woah, wow," he muttered. "Are you okay?"

"Yeah, I think so," I said. "It's all still…you know. A lot to take in."

That was when he took my hand. I gasped as another surge of electricity crackled between us. "I'm sorry," he said, squeezing it.

"Thanks," I mumbled, squeezing his back. It felt like he understood, *really* understood, in some deep-down way. Well, I guess his dad had let him down too.

We kept walking, and he didn't let go of my hand, and I didn't let go of his, all the way to the double doors.

School went okay. Marco didn't ask any more about my family. I think he got that I didn't want to talk about it, and that I wasn't keen on the others knowing just yet. There was no more spontaneous hand-holding (unfortunately!) but I managed to fix it to sit next to him at lunch, while making it look like it had just worked out that way.

Last lesson was the Media Diploma thing I'd signed up for. The teacher, Mr. Mac, was really nice, and young, and he talked to us in a normal way like we were just people and not *pupils*. Not everyone in our class was taking that option so there were only twelve of us, and we all got to sit round a big table together, like you would in sixth form.

We had to do a photography and design project to create a promotional leaflet or flyer for something, and we were actually going to have some printed up at the end by a professional press and go and get them displayed in shops and the information centre and the library and different places. We could work in pairs if we wanted and Summer instantly grabbed my hand, going, "Bags I'm with Abbie."

"Hey, I thought we were doing a promo for Headrush!" Marco complained.

She grinned. "We were, but actually I'm not that *into* the idea of following your band around, taking pictures. I don't want people thinking I'm one of the *fans*. Your head's big enough already."

Marco pulled a face at her and turned to Ben. "Looks like it's you and me then, mate. But you're not going to make me do, like, *nature*, are you?"

"I'm doing mine on the Estate Environmental Conservation Group at Dartington," Ben said. "I've already arranged to take the photos this weekend, when I'm volunteering."

"Oh, *good*," Marco grumbled. "I won't have to actually do any *conserving*, though, will I?"

Ben rolled his eyes. "Maybe I'll just go by myself, and you can write the leaflet text from my notes. Deal?"

Marco grinned. "Deal."

Me and Summer knew we wanted to do something different and cool, but we didn't know what. We were going to take each other's numbers and text when we got any inspiration, but then I remembered that my phone had stopped working the night before – like Saff's – so I made some excuse about how I couldn't get any coverage down here and I needed to change networks. I couldn't tell them what was really going on with us and money – it was way too scary, not to mention embarrassing (I didn't even tell *Marco* exactly how bad things were). I'd only just met them, and anyway, it was so nice to escape to school and just feel normal for a while.

For the rest of the lesson (well, *session*, as Mr. Mac called it), we looked at loads of examples of flyers, leaflets and promos that everyone had brought in and put in the middle of the table. We talked about how some of them had offers on, like getting two people in somewhere for the price of one, or details of a special event to go to, or a web page you could visit for news or to see a video. That way you kept hold of the flyer and didn't just chuck it away and forget about it. It was really cool, actually – I didn't know you could do this kind of stuff at school.

I was hoping Marco would ask me to the cafe again after the bell went. But even though I stood right next to him for ages, getting the stuff out of my locker as slowly as possible, he didn't. I guess I should have realized he'd lose interest pretty quickly – Summer and Ben had both made it clear to me what he was like.

And yet…when he'd pulled me out of the rain, there'd been an *extra-special* spark between us, I just knew it. And when we'd talked this morning, really talked, and he'd held my hand…there was a strong connection between us then, not just to do with his gorgeousness. But, urgh, did that mean I'd passed onto the *friend* list?

I was thinking about all this as I wandered home from school (on my own, as by the time I got to the gate, Grace had gone). I turned a corner into the quiet side street that leads out to our parade of shops on the main road, and saw a girl up ahead sitting on the pavement surrounded by stuff. *Loony alert*, I thought, and I was about to cross the road to avoid her when I realized it was Saff. She was sitting on our checked blanket amongst a pile of our wellies, with a few CDs, some sweets and a box of tissues in front of her, staring into space and looking like she was having some kind of crazy person's picnic.

"Saff, what—" I began.

"That's it, there really is nothing left now," she said, and burst into tears.

Suddenly I realized – the car had been parked here. We hadn't left it right near the flat in case the bailiffs traced it and found out where we were. I felt a wave of shock ripple through me – I could hardly believe this was all happening. But I bit my lip and swallowed it down. I had to be strong for Saff.

"Don't worry about it, it was just a car," I said.

Saff threw a welly into the road in frustration. "But it *wasn't* just a car, that's the point!" she wailed. "It was for me to learn to drive in, which was my passport back up to London, and my singing lessons, and my chance of being famous, of fulfilling my dream!"

Okay, so I could see why she was upset, but there was no point in me wallowing in misery with her. I sighed. "But Saff, all that's gone anyway. We don't have the money to put petrol in it, let alone for you to learn to drive or take singing lessons. It looks like you're going to have to make it to fame and fortune on your own."

Saff let out a loud sob. "What, without the right styling or any proper voice training? That's impossible!"

"Of course it's not," I insisted. "You can achieve anything if you try hard enough."

She grimaced. "Yeah, right."

"*Yes*. And think what a great story this will make when you're rich and famous. They love this kind of stuff on *The X Factor*. Imagine… Sapphire Green — abandoned by her father and penniless, the singing starlet had to flee her home and start a whole new life, overcoming hardship and beating the odds to achieve her dream."

Saff was silent for a while, then she said, "Maybe. I'd rather have the car back though, and a new wardrobe and shoes…" She sighed wistfully, imagining it all. "But I guess that really is gone now, so I don't have any choice."

"No, you don't," I said. "But luckily for you you'd look good in a bin bag." I narrowed my eyes at her.

She smiled wanly and took a tissue from the box, then dabbed at her running mascara and blew her nose. Then she looked right into my eyes, and she suddenly seemed so small and vulnerable. She still looked like Saff, but completely different too. "It will be okay, won't it, Abbie?" she asked.

I suddenly felt like the big sister.

What could I say? I just nodded, put my arm round her and squeezed her tight. But I couldn't get rid of the horrible churning feeling in my stomach. I mean, seriously, how *would* it be okay? There was no money for the rent, and time was running out. So I'd made some friends at my new school, but what was the point of that if I'd have to leave again next week?

I wondered what happens when you get chucked out on the street and you finally, actually, have *nothing* – no money and absolutely nowhere to go (and no car to go there in). Would they put us in a dodgy B&B somewhere that was even worse than the flat? I imagined a scary place with loud music and banging doors and people drinking and taking drugs.

Would we be split up? Would I have to move schools again? For a moment I thought of saying all that to Saff, to give her a reality check about her problem of not having the latest designer clothes. But I knew it wouldn't help. She was freaking out enough already. And I knew there was no point in me thinking about any of that either until it happened – *if* it happened.

So instead I picked up a welly. "Bet I can beat your throw," I said, hurling it into the road. It went just past hers.

"No way! Right, rematch!" she cried.

So we gathered up the wellies and shared them out fairly (i.e. we each got one of Dad's big, heavy ones) and took turns flinging them as hard as we could. When I picked up Dad's one I felt a bit sad for a moment, and wondered where he was, and what he was doing, and whether he was slipping around in the mud somewhere and needing them. Then I just felt really angry with him and threw the welly so hard, Saff cried, "Jeez, Abs, mind that parked car!"

After a while, all the wellies were in the road, and we'd been glared at by several passers-by, but at least my sister was smiling.

"Jelly baby?" I said, offering her the half-finished packet of sweets. That made us both giggle. A couple of ladies walked past just then and I realized what we must look like – two girls sitting on the pavement on a picnic blanket, eating jelly babies and having some kind of welly-throwing competition. "I thought the people were weird round here but they're nothing compared to us," I said.

Saff hugged me. "I don't think I could get through this without you, Abs," she said. "You're so strong."

That was nice of her. But for some reason it just made me feel really, really sick.

A little later, we tumbled into the flat, me with the picnic blanket like a sack over my shoulder with all the wellies in, like a really rubbish Father Christmas. Saff was clutching the tissue box and other bits. Grace was studying at the kitchen table and Mum was kneeling on the (now spotless) kitchen counter giving the window such a good clean that I said, "Are you trying to wipe the glass actually *off*?"

She smiled grimly. "No, I just thought it would be nice if we could see through it."

"I waited at the gate for you," Grace said to me.

"Yeah, sorry, I got held up," I replied, trying to keep my voice normal and not think about standing by my locker for ages like a lemon, hoping for another coffee invite from Marco that never came.

I let the blanket fall open and all the wellies clumped out onto the floor.

Grace looked up at last. "Why are you bringing those in?" she asked. "It's June. Surely it's better to leave them in the car? There's nowhere to put anything in this place."

Saff and I exchanged a glance then, and just as I was about to tell Grace what had happened, Mum surprised us by saying, "So I take it they came for the car, then?" She smiled grimly. "It was nice of them to leave the wellies. I'd forgotten about those."

Grace went pale. "What? But, if they've found the car, does that mean they know where we are? Are they going to come round here and try to take the rest of our stuff? Oh my gosh, those debt men are really scary, I've seen them on TV. They could be on their way here right now. We'd better bolt the door!"

When she said that, my heart started banging in my chest too, and Saff looked terrified.

Mum spoke all in a rush. "Grace, honey, calm down, it's okay. I rang the Range Rover showroom and told them where to find the car. I didn't give this address, of course not. No one is coming after us, I promise you."

Saff turned on Mum. "You rang them?" she screeched. "That car was the last thing we had! Even if we couldn't afford to keep it, we could have sold it and paid the rent for months ahead. And train tickets for me to go back to London. And new clothes. I could still have done my singing lessons. I don't *believe* this!"

Mum looked shaken. "It wasn't an easy decision, Saff," she half-whispered. "But I had to do the right thing. The car was on a credit agreement, so it didn't really belong to us. It got us down here in an

66

emergency, but keeping it after that would have been like stealing."

"Look around, Mum, it still *is* an emergency," Saff snapped, then went into full flouncy sulk mode and stormed off to the bathroom.

I put the kettle on and made tea for everyone, like I used to at home. I know it's weird but I love the smell of the steam coming up when you pour the water on, especially if it's Earl Grey or lapsang souchong (not that we had any of that here).

Mum came over to get her mug and paused for a moment. "Oh, Abbie, you've made five, love," she said, looking startled.

"Oh, yeah. My brain's zapped from school," I mumbled. But we both knew I'd automatically made one for Dad.

Mum squeezed my shoulders and gave me a sad smile, but she didn't say anything about it, thank goodness. Just tipping it down the sink seemed too awful somehow, like I was tipping Dad down with it, so I drank mine, then gulped his down too, even though I didn't really want it. Grace was buried in her homework at the table by then, and Saff was out of her mood and looking at the free paper with Mum.

As I pretended to read one of my soap-making recipe books on the sofa, I couldn't help wondering what Dad was doing right now. Was he thinking about me like I was thinking about him? Was he worried about us? I wished that he could ring us, or that I had a number for him, so I could let him know we were okay, at least.

Then I glanced at my family — Grace frowning over her books, Saff circling job ads in the paper, Mum's face a mask of worry. Suddenly I felt guilty for even *wanting* to speak to him. It felt like I was betraying them. But then, we weren't going to just forget about him, were we?

I wanted to talk to Mum about it, but it didn't seem like the right time. So, for the moment, I put it all at the back of my mind and went to get my box of beauty ingredients. I had just about enough essential oils left to make some solid perfume. I planned to fill the kitchen with the scents of rose and geranium, and maybe a bit of sweet orange and bergamot too. They're supposed to be uplifting. I doubted they were uplifting enough to make us all feel totally better about the future, but maybe their warm cosy glow swirling around us would be enough to lift the cloud of gloom just a little.

* * *

On Friday just before lunch I was putting some books back in my locker and someone leaned in close to me, sending a shiver right through me.

"Hmm, nice smell," he said.

I knew that voice. But I should have realized it was Marco *before* he spoke. Who else would make me go all trembly like that? I had to reduce the wattage on my grin before I turned round though, so that he didn't think I was some kind of loony.

"It's solid perfume, I made it myself," I said, showing him the little vintage compact I'd put it in. "I like making beauty products." He looked a bit blank, so I added, "You know, face masks, moisturizers, bath foam…"

"Oh, right, like, girl stuff," he said gruffly.

"Men should moisturize too, you know," I told him, acting all stern. I leaned right up to him and peered at his skin. "Hmm, yes, I can already see some fine lines and wrinkles…"

He grinned. "Oh yeah?"

"Yeah. Look, here…" I brushed his cheek lightly with my finger. Honestly, I had to use every ounce of my willpower to stop myself from trying to kiss him there and then.

Just then, Summer came striding up, and I leaped backwards and tried to look normal. She spotted the compact, took it from me and had a big sniff. "Ooooh, that's gorgeous!" she cried. "Where did you get it?"

"I made it," I said.

"OMG, wow!" she squealed.

"OMG, wow!" copied Marco, in an even more girly way, and headed for the lunch hall before Summer could slap him one.

"I *love* this. Can you make me one?" she cried. "Where did you get the little case?"

"Oh, I pick them up from junk shops, vintage fairs. I used to go down to Portobello Road market all the time," I said. "I've got a few left at home. Course I can do you one."

Summer grinned at me. "Thanks. It's amazing you can make this stuff. You're so talented!"

"Oh, yes, I'm just amazing, me!" I joked. As we linked arms and set off down the corridor, I felt all warm and glowy inside. I hadn't felt that way for ages. Summer liking the perfume and wanting one had given me that real boost I used to get, like when I made stuff for Em and Zo and I could see they really loved it.

Thinking of them made me desperate for one of our long girly three-way Skype chats, but then I remembered I didn't have a phone. Mum had bought one of those pay-as-you-go ones for a fiver from the supermarket the day before, but that was strictly so people could call her about jobs, and she'd put a pound on it in case she had to ring a doctor or something.

And anyway, even if I had an iPhone with video link, what would I say to them? I'd have to tell them about everything that had happened, and how we might soon be completely homeless. For some reason, I just felt like they wouldn't understand. But strangely enough, I found myself wanting to tell Summer and Ben. Some of it, anyway. And I soon got my chance.

What happened was we were all sitting around at lunch, and I must have been off in my own world, because suddenly Summer was going, "Earth to Abbie? Are your parents cool with you coming to His Maj's gig, then?"

"Par*ent*," I said, and then it all came out.

Of course, Summer wasn't going to be happy with just one sentence, like Marco had been. She wanted to know all the details, about the affair, and the family conference, and Mum and Dad splitting up. I told them as much as I knew, and it was a relief, actually, to talk about it.

"Oh my gosh!" gasped Summer. "You poor thing! I wish you'd told us sooner!"

Marco just gave me a sad smile.

"So what are you doing down here then?" Ben asked, looking a bit shocked.

"My dad's business went under and we lost our house," I croaked. In my mind I saw the image of us throwing our stuff into suitcases and bags, with no idea of what was really going on, thinking we were basically off on a long luxury holiday. If I'd known I'd never see the place again, or my stuff, I'd have brought pink rabbit with me. He was only a tattered pyjama case, but I'd had him since I was about four. I know it was stupid, but thinking about him sitting there on my shelf (if he still was), or in our old neighbours' garage shoved in a box, or worse, chucked away in a bin bag somewhere, got me all choked up and I couldn't finish speaking.

Summer put her arm round me. "Oh, you poor thing," she said. "How did that happen?"

But I still couldn't get any words out. Suddenly what had happened between Mum and Dad seemed too awful, and overwhelming, and I didn't want to talk about it any more.

"You look like you could do with an iced bun," said Marco.

"That would be nice," I said. I smiled gratefully at him and he smiled back at me. Then he got up and headed for the counter. It was nice, too, that he hadn't let on to Ben and Summer that he'd already known about my family situation. *And* he'd kept it just between us since I'd told him. He'd let *me* decide when I was ready to talk to them about it.

Summer was doing the goggly-eyes thing at Ben. "Good thinking about buns," he said suddenly, shooting out of his seat. He gave me such a sympathetic smile I almost burst into tears, and then he went after Marco.

I leaned in to Summer. "I'm okay now, but thanks for being so lovely," I said.

"Well, if you ever want to talk——" she began.

"Thanks," I said quickly, cutting her off. "I just want to forget about it for now though." I knew I had to compose myself *right away*, or there was a danger I'd lose it completely and have to go round all day crying like a total wreck. Which would play havoc with my mascara.

"Okay, if you're sure," she said then.

"I'm sure," I insisted.

She followed my gaze to where I was accidentally staring at Marco. "You two were acting weird by the lockers just now... Is something going on between you?"

Bless her for changing the subject even though I

could see she was still worried about me. "I don't know, is it?" I asked. "You know him really well. You tell me."

"Abbie!" she gasped, staring at me wide-eyed.

"I mean, no it's not!" I hissed, back-pedalling. "Nothing's going on…"

But she stood up and pulled me with her. "Right. Me. You. Loos. Now," she said, and I was marched off.

"Summer, I don't know why you dragged me in here!" I protested, when we were in front of the mirrors, pretending to check our hair. "There's nothing to say! I really like him, that's all… As a friend…"

Her eyes bored into mine. She wasn't buying any of it.

"Okay, I admit it, I have a huge bone-shaking crush on him!" I cried. "Are you happy now?"

She gave a long sigh. "No, not really. Ben said he gave you the heads-up about Marco already, or I would have said something myself."

"I can't help how I feel," I said, a bit snottily.

"Well, *try*," she countered. "Five words: Lucy. Ruby. Rachel. Sharmin. Alesha. Those are all the girls he's led on then messed about in the last few months. No, hang on, six words: Gabrielle."

"Okay, okay, I get the picture," I grumbled.

Summer frowned, thinking. "No, actually, seven, because there was Charlise as well. I forgot about her because she's in Year 11."

"Year 11!" I screeched, then managed to compose myself. "Look, it's irrelevant because I don't think he likes me anyway," I said. I secretly thought he might, but I wanted to see her reaction.

"It's obvious he does," she countered, and I had to concentrate really hard to stop myself from breaking into a happy dance. "Has he said anything?" she asked then.

"No. Well, not really. He asked me for coffee once but I couldn't go and he hasn't said anything since."

Summer looked gleeful. "You knocked him back?" she cried. "Hee hee! That serves him right!"

"I didn't *mean* to. I didn't even know if he meant it as a just me-and-him thing or if other people would be there or whatever, and Grace was waiting for me and—"

"He must have been gutted!" she squealed. "Oh, I so can't wait to tell Ben about this!"

I must have looked a bit annoyed then because she stopped mucking around. "Look, seriously, Abs, I'm telling you this as a friend. I've known Marco for ever, and I love him to bits. Underneath the Romeo act he's the same boy I've been mates with for years. He's kind and funny and thoughtful. But since his dad left town the last time, halfway through last year, well, I don't know... It's like he thinks he's got something to prove. He seems to like a girl, and they get really close, and maybe even start going out, then BANG, he goes cold just like that."

"Yeah, but I—" I began, but she cut me off.

"Look, he's my mate and I don't like talking about him like this, but you're my friend too, and I don't want to see you get hurt, that's all."

"Don't worry, I won't," I promised her, putting on a smile. I could see how it looked, and I didn't want to seem like a total doormat. "I can look after myself. I'm a London girl, innit?" I added, doing a rude-girl voice.

"Good," said Summer.

Secretly, though, I believed that it *was* different for me and Marco. We had such a strong connection. That moment when we'd held hands walking along, it was like we just totally understood each other, without even having to say anything. He couldn't have had *that* with seven other girls, surely?

"Hey, how about we go shopping tomorrow?" Summer was saying as she pushed the door open.

"I can show you this great place——"

"Oh, thanks, but I can't," I said quickly. "I'm planning to go and explore the town with Mum and my sisters. You know, have a proper look around. Another time, though."

"Okay, cool, no worries," she said. "Check out Willow when you stop for lunch, it's this yummy veggie restaurant. And listen, get your network changed soon, yeah? I can't even get *hold* of you outside school! We still need to sort out our Media project."

"Yeah, sure, I will," I said. It gave me a start though, remembering that, even after the talk we'd just had, none of my new friends knew *exactly* what an awful situation we were in now, money-wise. However much I'd told them, I hadn't been able to bring myself to say we had nothing, and that if a job didn't come along soon for Mum or Saff we could be out on the streets in a matter of days. Still, maybe they'd find something at the weekend, or our benefits would come through, and the rent would be paid in time. Maybe, after a while, we could even put enough aside to do up the flat a bit. Then I'd feel like I could bring people round. If all that happened, there'd be nothing to actually *tell*.

"Are you sure you're okay?" Summer was asking.

I shrugged. "Well, you know, it's not easy, but—"

"Any time you want to talk, just ring me, okay? I'll come straight over."

"Okay, thanks." She hugged me and I must have felt a bit better, because I managed to hug her back without bursting into tears. Then we headed back into the lunch hall.

As we neared our table, Marco finished off his own iced bun and reached for mine, so I swiped it off his plate. "Hey, that's supposed to be for me!" I cried. "I'm upset, remember?"

He raised his eyebrows. "Well, you look alright to me," he said, with a cheeky smile. "More than alright."

I tried not to blush at that, and I deliberately didn't look at Summer.

As we all chatted and joked, I kept sneaking glances at him, wondering whether Summer's words would have somehow magically changed how I felt. He flicked his hair from his eyes and my stomach jolted. *Nope.*

The good thing was, I knew what he was like, so I wouldn't fall into the same trap as those other girls did, would I? I could have a laugh with him, see if he did really like me, see what happened, see if I *was* different. Make sure this connection I felt we had was real before I got involved. I could hold the cards and call the shots and all those kind of phrases. There was no danger I'd end up being Broken Heart Number 8, was there?

Chapter Four

Mum, Saff, Grace and I were actually feeling quite positive when we left the flat to head into town on Saturday morning. We'd all used my lemon zest shower gel to give us some extra zing and my olive grain foot scrub seemed to have put a spring in Mum's step. She and Saff had dressed up smartly, and planned to ask about jobs as we went round town (well, check back to see if anything had come up, in Mum's case).

As we piled out of the door, Saff and Grace were busy arguing as usual, this time over whether Grace's skirt went with her shoes (Saff said it didn't and Grace said she didn't care). They soon stopped when we saw the big, muscle-bound man holding a Price Cutter bag and unlocking the door to the next flat along. He gave us a friendly grin and said, "Morning. I take it you've just moved in."

"Yes," said Mum. "I'm Kim, nice to meet you. And these are my daughters, Sapphire, Grace and Abbie."

"Hello," we chorused.

"Nice to meet you all, too," he said. "I'm Liam. You should come round for a cup of tea sometime, once you're settled." Mum said thank you, and invited him round to our flat too (lucky, lucky man!). Then he added, "And if there's anything you need…"

"Four iPhones," I thought to myself, "a laptop and wireless broadband, a car, new school uniforms, jobs for Mum and Saff, a decent flat… If it's not too much trouble, of course."

As Mum cried, "Abbie, for goodness' sake!" and steered me away, I realized I'd said that out loud. Argh. I *have* to stop doing that.

Well, apart from that, our trip into town started off well. We found this cool place called Vire Island that's in the middle of the river, and from there we walked over the bridge and all the way up Fore Street and the high street (past Willow, the restaurant

Summer had mentioned), looking at all the cool little shops and cafes.

But by the time we got to the castle at the top of town, our feet wcrc dragging and our mood had crashed. Everyone had been nice and taken Saff's details, but no one had said there was actually any work going at the moment, and it was the same when Mum checked back with people. Saff isn't exactly great with rejection at the best of times, and she got more and more grumpy, until Mum said it was time to stop asking because the way she was just slouching into places was actually giving a *bad* impression. Grace even asked about summer work in a couple of places, but it seemed like they only wanted over sixteens.

I thought my heart would explode from watching Mum pull herself together, reset her smile and go into each place as if it was the first, but after a long string of "no"s even she was beginning to look tired and defeated. We sat down on the sloping grass near the castle and I put my arm round her. "We've still got a few days to come up with the rent," I said. "And Saturday probably isn't the best day for this kind of thing – everyone's really busy and the weekend staff don't know anything about what jobs are going. Come back up on Monday, it'll be better then." I wasn't sure I really believed that, but I had to say something to cheer her up.

Luckily she gave me a small smile. "Maybe you're right," she said. "Look, let's get an ice cream each – we can just about afford that – and then we can go into the information centre on the way back to the flat and get some leaflets about country trails."

"What, you mean, so we can go on a *walk*?" gasped Saff.

"Don't look so horrified," said Mum. "The flat's only a stone's throw from open country. There'll be some nice routes we don't need to drive to. There's no point being in beautiful Devon if we're not going to see any of it."

"And walks are free," said Grace approvingly. "We can stop back at the flat first and make some sandwiches as well, to save buying lunch out."

"Urgh, not more cheese spread," groaned Saff, rolling her eyes.

She got on board with the plan eventually, though, and a couple of hours later we had dodged some scary-looking cows, had hysterics watching her trying to climb over a stile, and saved Grace from a wasp that she was convinced was *deliberately* chasing her. Soon we were sitting on top of a big hill in the sunshine, scoffing our sandwiches, and no one was complaining about the cheese spread.

We got really silly then, because Saff decided that as no one was around we were all going to do the Macarena and sing at the tops of our voices. For those few minutes, we were just completely carried away having fun and we forgot about everything. Then Grace spotted a couple of dog walkers coming our way and we had to try and act sensible.

That night we watched a film and everything was still kind of okay. It was like all the fun and fresh air we'd had on the hill had made us immune to the depressing grottiness of the flat. But the effect wore off overnight, and on Sunday morning we woke up to pouring rain, and it felt like the gloom was going to settle back over us again.

That was, until I got my stuff out to make the solid perfume I'd promised Summer. I could have just given her one of the compacts I'd made the other night, of course, but I'd decided to create a blend of essential oils especially for her. Instead of letting me get on with it on my own like normal, Saff offered to help, and then Mum and Grace came and got involved too. In the end, everyone wanted their own signature scent and we had all my oils out on the table, passing the bottles round and trying different combinations, smelling each other's blends and making suggestions, experimenting and adjusting.

I settled on bergamot, jasmine and geranium for Summer (I'd decided that the geranium and rose I'd made for myself was going to become *my* signature scent after Marco liked it so much, so I wasn't making her *exactly* the same one!). I chose a lovely enamelled compact for her, and Mum, Saff and Grace chose one each too.

We made up names for our perfumes and I wrote them on each compact in swirly writing with silver pen. I called Summer's "Summer Breeze" and decided that mine would be "Wild Rose".

It was really nice, sitting round the table with endless cups of tea, making stuff together. So nice, in fact, that they helped me make a batch of lavender bath bombs too, and some lime and ginger body scrub (only half a batch, though, as I'd nearly used up all the Dead Sea salt and ginger essential oil I had left).

I hoped my ingredients for making products wouldn't run out too soon, as there was no way I could afford to buy any more, of course. And I was getting the feeling that my special box of oils and creams, bases and natural colourings, flower petals and herbs was somehow more than just a bunch of stuff to make beauty products with. That afternoon, it became like some kind of special sweet-smelling, reviving, swirling magic that kept us going.

Summer went crazy over the little perfume compact when I gave it to her on the field at morning break on Monday. So she must have been surprised when I burst into tears. Ben and Marco certainly were. We were all lazing about on the grass – luckily I'd found a fiver in one of my jeans pockets the night before, which had meant I could buy an organic apple juice and rice cakes so they wouldn't start asking questions about money. But it didn't matter in the end, because I just wasn't able to hide it all any more.

Summer was saying how amazing the perfume was, Ben was having a look at the compact and Marco was just lying in the sun, giving me a slow, lazy (possibly flirty?) smile. Just looking at them all and thinking that I'd probably have to leave them in a few days' time made me realize how close we'd got, and I felt really gutted. That's what the crying was about.

When they saw the tears, Marco shot up and asked if I was okay, Summer put her arm round me, and Ben just looked really concerned. So it all came out then — about how Mr. Vulmer would be round on Wednesday and we didn't have the rent money. "There are only two days left to find it and after that we'll be made homeless, and I'll have to leave the school and I really like it here, and it's not fair because I've only just met you guys," I finished breathlessly.

"Oh, Abbie, you poor thing," Summer cried. "But listen, we won't let that happen," she insisted, wrapping me up in a huge hug. "I know Mum and Dad haven't got any spare cash to lend, but you can all come and stay with us for as long as you like."

That was so nice, it just made me cry even more. "Thanks, but we couldn't possibly…" I began.

"Of course you could," she insisted. "Jim and Jed can share, or you can have the yurt we've got in the field." I couldn't help smiling at that — the idea of *Sapphire* living in basically a glorified *tent*.

"I'd love to offer as well, but you couldn't swing a cat in our place," said Ben. "Not that I'd try to, obviously."

He always knew how to make me smile. "Thanks for the thought, anyway," I told him.

I realized then that they were both looking at Marco. He hadn't said anything, and they obviously thought he should have done. Argh! I really wanted them to stop it. It was making me feel completely stupid and my blush-ometer was going off the scale. I hadn't expected any of them to offer anything. But now that Marco wasn't, and not even explaining why not, like Ben did, Miss Paranoid here was wondering why. Maybe he was still annoyed about the knock-back (if it even *was* a knock-back, if the coffee was even a *thing* in the first place) or maybe he found the thought of me, wandering around in the night with no make-up on looking headless, far too terrifying.

"Ooooh, wouldn't you want Abbie to see you without your cool gear and hair gel on?" Summer teased.

I thought he'd flick her the Vs as usual, but instead he just blushed and looked really flustered. "Course you can stay with us, Abs," he mumbled.

I felt an even bigger rush of blood to my cheeks and stared hard at the grass. One thought had led to another and suddenly I was imagining us living under the same roof, chatting late at night, cooking together, watching DVDs… But then…I'd have to sneakily get up at 5 a.m. every day to do my make-up, ditch my awful too-short puppy PJs and obviously I'd never *ever* be able to do a number two.

So maybe it wouldn't be such a great option after all.

I glanced up and caught his eye. An intense look passed between us. I don't know what was in *his* head, but he still looked as flustered as I did. Was that a good sign? I wasn't sure.

"It's really, really nice of you all," I said, smiling a little. "I'm sure that, even if the worst did happen, we'd be able to sort something out, but just knowing you're there for me means such a lot."

Summer squeezed my shoulders. "You're not going anywhere," she said firmly. "We won't let you."

That was so nice of her, but unless she had some kind of magic power I didn't know about, I didn't see what she could really do about it.

We had netball after lunch, and no one minded that I didn't have a proper kit (I'd just taken some shorts and a T-shirt – no way was I making last week's uniform mistake again. Even if Marco was into me now, he wouldn't be if he saw me trotting out in a pea-green PE skirt, complete with matching humungous gym knickers and an Aertex top with Abigail Green embroidered across the front).

I really enjoyed pounding around on the court with my mind completely focussed on the game – it was lovely not thinking about all our problems. And a couple of girls on my team, Olivia and Rose, said I was really good. It was a boiling hot day, so after the game I went in the showers, but I made sure I kept my face out of the water so my make-up didn't get ruined. I wasn't planning on a repeat of the headless look.

I got out my home-made hand cream and body lotion afterwards and Summer wanted to try them, and then Jess did, and suddenly there was a whole crowd of girls round me. They all loved the products (I let them have a bit each). Then Summer got her perfume compact out too to show them and they all went on about how gorgeous it was. When Mrs. Lurman came over to see what the fuss was about, I thought we might get told off but she had a try too.

"Mmm, this hand cream smells delicious," she enthused. "If you're making a new batch, put me down for some too. You'll have to let me know how much it is."

The girls wanted me to "put them down" for things too, and they were asking about prices and what else I could make. It should have been really cool and exciting, but instead it just made me feel really stressed out, because I had to nod and go "yeah" and say I'd let them know. The truth was, I didn't have enough money to buy any more ingredients, and my stocks were too low to start turning out new batches of stuff.

I told Mum, Saff and Grace about it when I got home.

"I wish I could magic the money up for you, hon," Mum said, "because I'm sure you'd make it back again, and more. But we've hardly got enough for food. I've been on to the jobcentre again about our benefits, but it all takes time."

"And there's no news about jobs for me, either," said Saff gloomily. "I went back round everywhere today, and made sure I spoke to the managers, and yes, I did wear my happy face, Grace, but it's the same as Mum found – everyone's taken on their summer staff already."

"It's so unfair," Grace grumbled. "I'm more mature than most sixteen-year-olds, but it seems like no one will even *consider* me for a summer job."

Mum sighed. "I don't want to upset you girls even more, but I'm afraid I've seen the R-A-T again."

That was the final straw for Saff. She collapsed onto the revolting brown sofa (which was a bit less revolting since Mum had spread one of her huge Hermes scarves over the back of it) with her head in her hands, groaning.

"Oh, thanks, you could have told me!" Grace moaned, pushing her chair out from the table and pulling her knees up under her chin.

"It was hours ago now. It ran across here and in there and it hasn't been out all afternoon," said Mum, pointing at a hole in the skirting board. "Still, I've mopped the floor anyway." She shuddered. "Twice. But don't worry, I'm going to ask Liam — you know, the neighbour we met — to come round and get rid of it."

Grace looked horrified. "Mum!" she shrieked. "That's so sexist, just assuming that he can deal with the rat because he's a man and we can't because we're women."

"I'll take that to mean *you'll* kill it for us then," said Mum, reaching for the broom and leaning it on the table beside Grace. "Sorry we don't have anything heavier to clunk it on the head with," she added, "you'll just have to hit it *really* hard. Then you'll need to pick it up and bury it outside, oh and block up the hole afterwards."

Grace gave her a surly look.

"No?" said Mum breezily. "I didn't think so. Put the kettle on then, I'll be back in a minute." And with that she ruffled her hair, smoothed down her top and skirt, and swanned out.

She came back a few minutes later with Liam in tow. He was so big and muscly that he filled the whole doorway, and he was carrying a spade. He looked scarier than I remembered, until he walked in and gave us all a big warm smile, and said, "Hello, ladies. I hear you've got a problem."

I felt like I ought to lean over to Saff and shut her mouth for her, because it was hanging open again. Grace seemed completely immune to Liam though, and just said a quick hello, then went back to her room to study.

After teas all round, Mum, Saff and I went and sat on the slightly-less-revolting brown sofa to wait for the rat. It didn't take long, as it turned out. As soon as we were quiet, it came out after the bit of cheese Liam had put on the floor. We all screamed and scrambled onto the back of the sofa, with our feet on the seat and our fists in our mouths, eyes squeezed shut, waiting for the fatal blow.

But, instead of despatching the rat (to, erm…rat heaven?), Liam screamed too.

"Hit it with the spade!" Saff coached unhelpfully as he danced from foot to foot.

"I can't, I can't! It's massive!" he squealed.

The rat looked just as panicked as us by this point and went to run back into the skirting board, but Liam brought the spade crashing down, blocking the hole, and the rat started running round the kitchen instead.

"Kim, open the front door!" Liam shrieked. "Come on, quick! And Abbie, run downstairs and open the main door!"

I felt like saying, "Erm, hang on, why can't Saff go?" but I just leaped up and bolted for the stairs – I didn't fancy being halfway down them when the rat came scurrying past me. As I ran, I heard Liam screech, "Sapphire, go and close the other doors and I'll herd it past you," and I decided I'd got the better job after all.

There was a lot of screaming and swatting and thumping around from above, and the next minute the rat came shooting past me and scampered away into the nearest bush. I slammed the door and raced upstairs, my heart pounding.

Back in the kitchen, we were all trembling and giddy and in near hysterics – re-enacting all the leaping about and teasing each other about how freaked out we'd been.

When we'd calmed down, Liam sealed up the rat hole with a manky old breadboard we found in the Hoover cupboard. He said he'd pop back soon with some humane traps in case there were any more, and a new bit of skirting board to finish the job properly. Mum couldn't thank him enough and somehow it felt like we'd known him far longer than half an hour. He ended up staying for dinner, which was cannelloni, but without the expensive crème fraîche or mozzarella or basil (so tomato pasta, basically). Still, he kept saying how nice it was and what a good cook Mum was. Then, after we'd eaten, we sat round the table chatting for ages (well, apart from Grace, who sneaked off again to study). Mum gave Liam a cleaned-up account of what had happened back in Ealing and why we'd moved into the flat, with Saff throwing in barbed comments about Dad.

Then while Mum was getting the kettle on, Liam had another look at the breadboard-covered rat-hole. "You know, it's probably best to replace that whole piece of skirting board, Kim," he said. "I've got some offcuts from my last job that should colour match okay. I'll measure up and trim them down to size, and it's sorted."

Mum was looking confused. "From your last job?" she repeated. "What do you do?"

"I'm a builder."

"A builder?" she cried. "But that's so…I mean…" She blushed the colour of the tomato pasta then. "Oh sorry, I just assumed…"

"What, that because I'm gay I must be a hairdresser or something?" he teased.

"Well, you weren't exactly manly about the rat!" Saff fired in.

"Oooh, get you!" Liam cried, pretending to be really camp. "Actually, building isn't the greatest career for me at the moment," he said then. "My back's really been playing up the last few months, especially with all the lifting I have to do. I've been in agony most nights."

"Oh, you poor thing. I could give you a massage," Mum offered. Then she blushed again. "Sorry, that sounded a bit odd. I mean, I'm a qualified massage therapist. I might be a little bit rusty, but you never forget the basics. And I'd love to do something for you, in return for sorting out the R-A-T situation."

"That would be amazing," Liam said eagerly. "If you're sure."

"Of course I am," Mum insisted. "We could do it right now." She pressed her hands down on the table. "I think this will hold you, and we can make it a bit nicer in here…"

Mum, Saff and I sprung into action then. I went and got the rest of the massage oil I'd mixed up recently for Mum's shoulders – it was a nice warming spicy one with cinnamon, clove and frankincense, just the thing for relaxing knotty muscles. Saff found some emergency candles for power cuts under the sink, and we stood a few along the counter in washed-out tomato tins.

Then me and Saff made ourselves uncomfortable on the revolting brown sofa and read magazines as Mum got started. Liam seemed to be enjoying it in general, but we couldn't help bursting out laughing because every time Mum touched a sore spot he shrieked like a banshee.

"For a big bloke, you're a bit of a weed," Saff sniggered.

"He's being very brave," said Mum kindly. "His back's in a terrible mess."

I felt really proud of her then. There she was, really making a difference to Liam, using this amazing skill we'd almost forgotten she had. And she didn't have that nervous, worried look on her face any more. She was deep in concentration, working her magic, and she just seemed really relaxed. After a while, Liam stopped screeching and seemed to go into some kind of coma, and a bubble of calm surrounded them both.

When Mum finally finished, he thanked her about a million times and declared that he felt like a new man. He also said Mum deserved a drink after all her efforts, so he popped over to his flat and came back with a bottle of wine.

I went off to read my mag in our room after that, but I had to go into the kitchen a couple of times to get stuff. Each time I noticed that the bottle had less wine in, the emergency candles were burning lower and Mum and Liam were discussing the total rubbishness of men even more loudly.

Not that I was listening or anything, but apparently Liam is on his own too now, because someone he called The Egotistical Brazilian Ballroom Dancer dumped him a few weeks ago for The Arrogant Scottish Skiing Instructor. The last thing I saw was Mum leaning right over the table, trying to tell him that the two of them both sounded utterly horrible and deserved each other, but not being able to pronounce the name of either. I decided it was time to go to bed then.

Chapter Five

Tuesday was pretty awful. Mum woke up with a banging headache, Saff said she felt too depressed to even get dressed, let alone go out to ask about work, and Grace just looked like she was going to burst into tears at any moment. The gloom cloud hanging over us was so big now, it was going to take more than a jar of perfume or a shower with some almond shell body scrub to cut through it. I hardly saw the point of going to school, what with our landlord's deadline looming, but I did anyway, because it was better than hanging round the flat being miserable all day.

Summer kept giving me tragic looks in our lessons, and at break she asked me about ten times if I wanted to talk about things. I really didn't but she wouldn't get the hint, so at lunchtime I made an excuse to stay in and skulked round the library instead of hanging out with her and the boys. I grabbed my stuff and hurried straight off after school too, and for once I didn't even think about whether Marco might ask me for coffee ever again or not. I had way bigger things to worry about.

Mr. Vulmer would be back for the rent tomorrow, and we just didn't have it. I walked home with Grace trailing along silently beside me, and when we got back into the flat, none of us even talked about jobs turning up or benefits arriving in the nick of time. We were beaten – and we knew it. This time tomorrow night we'd probably be in emergency housing – a B&B somewhere, or worse, a homeless shelter. Summer's yurt was beginning to seem quite appealing. Liam had offered for us to stay at his, but he only had one bedroom, so we'd all be in the lounge (although he'd probably insist on sleeping on the sofa and giving us his room). I wondered if we'd have to split up – me and Grace at Summer's and Mum and Saff at Liam's. I decided that would be worse than all being together in a horrible B&B somewhere. Our family had been fractured enough already.

In the end, I had a bath to try and escape the gloom cloud in the kitchen. I lit a yummy-scented candle, filled the tub with hot water and lashings of my warm spicy orange, cinnamon and geranium bath foam and smoothed an avocado face pack onto my skin. I got in, laid back, closed my eyes and tried to pretend I was still in our posh bathroom in Ealing. Then my mind began to drift and I started thinking about how much Summer had loved the solid perfume I made her, and how excited the girls at school and Mrs. Lurman had been over my creams and lotions, and about Mum giving Liam that massage and us all making those essential oil blends together on Sunday...

I opened my eyes a little and gazed at my home-made lotions, foams, oils, creams, scrubs, gels and butters, all lined up along the side of the bath. They each had their own properties, like magic potions – the power to make you feel relaxed or revived or uplifted, some pizzazz to wake you up in the morning or little bit of heaven at the end of a long day...and not forgetting a cool, fresh peppermint lip balm – for perfectly kissable lips...

Suddenly everything came together in my head. And in that second, I had it – the solution to all our problems.

By the time I was dry and rubbing the last of my avocado body butter into my legs, I'd worked the whole thing out. I strode out of the bathroom in a cloud of steam and delicious smells, straight into the kitchen. Everyone was sitting at the table – Grace just staring at her maths workbook without seeing anything, Mum tapping her fingernails on the pay-as-you-go phone that never rang, and Saff flicking listlessly through a magazine.

"I've got an idea," I announced. They all looked up, surprised. I couldn't stop grinning. "We'll set up our own beauty parlour in the empty shop downstairs. I'll create the products to sell, and use in our treatments – all natural and freshly home-made, of course. And we can do smoothies too, so it's about looking after yourself on the inside as well. There must be business loans for this kind of thing. Mum, you and Saff can run it full-time, at least until your course starts, Saff. Grace can handle the budgets and accounts and all that stuff. Oh, and I've just thought, me and Summer can photograph the products and make a promotional leaflet as our Media project."

They were all just staring at me, like I was speaking Japanese.

Finally Mum spoke. "Well, wow, Abbie. It's a good idea but, I don't know... With things as they are at the moment… Setting up a small business is a massive risk, especially in this climate when people just aren't spending. Not that we've even got the capital to start up, and as if that pig landlord would let us use the shop! I know you're trying to help, love, but it just sounds like chasing rainbows to me."

Chasing rainbows. That was one of Mum's phrases. It meant chasing an impossible dream.

But my dream wasn't impossible, was it?

"Surely anything's possible, if you try hard enough?" I asked her. "That's what you always told us when we were little."

Mum blinked at me. "I did used to say that, didn't I?"

"It's not chasing rainbows," I said firmly. "It's the beginning of a whole new adventure. It could bring us the pot of gold we need and be a proper new start. Not just surviving, but really living. Getting our lives back – not our old ones, but brand-new ones. It could make all our dreams come true."

"Cool!" cried Saff. "Let's do it!"

"We could look into the figures," said Grace. "Maybe talk to the bank. There's nothing to lose in that."

"And if we explain our plans to Mr. Vulmer and say we'll have the money soon, maybe…" Saff added.

We all looked at Mum. "Oh, I don't know – maybe I am being too negative," she said. "Things have been so easy, so comfortable, for the last few years. Bigger house, better car, smarter area, more time, more money. Not that I'm complaining, of course. But, when it all came crashing down, I didn't know what to do. I used to be so capable. Maybe I've lost something since those times. You're right, Abbie – nothing's impossible."

I grinned at her. "Thanks, Mum."

"And besides," she added, "they do say you should only start a business in an area you understand, and what I don't know about spa treatments isn't worth knowing!"

"Too right – you've spent half your life in those places!" I teased.

"Erm, Abs—" Grace began, but Saff cut in, saying, "We could have cool pink uniforms and—"

"Abs!" shrieked Grace, as the bathroom lit up brightly behind me. The hand towel had caught fire! Turns out Grace had been trying to tell me that my candle (home-made of course, uplifting jasmine and bergamot) looked a bit too close to it. We all screamed and dashed into the bathroom, where Mum flicked the burning towel into the bath water and snapped the light on.

She looked cross for a moment but then she started to laugh. "I always said you'd set the world on fire, Abbie," she gasped. "I just didn't think you'd start with the bathroom!"

Later on, when Liam popped round to fit the new bit of skirting board, I told him about my idea. I only mentioned it to chat, but amazingly he said, "That sounds brilliant. I'll help you fit out the shop, if you like."

I thought Mum would be pleased but instead she just looked flustered. "Oh, Liam, that's an amazing offer," she said, "but I'm afraid it's all just dreams and ideas at the moment. We don't have any money to get started, and I very much doubt the bank would consider lending us any. In fact, we don't even have the rent for this place, which means that by this time tomorrow we'll be evicted." She sighed. "So I'm not sure why I spent so long cleaning those windows," she added, trying to make him laugh, but looking as though she was about to cry.

Liam looked really worried. "That won't happen," he said, but he didn't sound convinced. "And if it does, like I said, you can all crash at mine till you sort things out. As for the beauty parlour, it's a fantastic idea, and you mustn't give up on it. If you can pull something out of the hat cash-wise, I'll do the shop fit for the cost of the materials. I've been using the same suppliers for years – I can call in a few favours, get some really good discounts."

Mum blinked at him. Then something happened that none of us were expecting. She threw her arms round him and burst into tears.

He hugged her back. "Kim, hon, I'm trying to cheer you up, not upset you!"

Mum pulled away and smoothed her blouse down, suddenly self-conscious. "You *are* cheering me up!" she insisted. "Honestly! I'm so sorry, it's just… this is exactly what we need, a bit of support. Even if this beauty parlour idea never gets off the ground, it's so nice to feel that we're not on our own." Then she giggled, and burst into tears again. "I'm sorry," she sniffled, "I mean, we've only known you a few days. I'm being ridiculous."

"No, you're not," said Liam. "You've been through a lot. Try and look at coming here as an exciting new start, yeah? And I'm your first new friend."

"Bleurgh!" Saff shuddered. "Have I accidentally walked into a musical? Are you two going to start singing or something?"

Mum sniffed and smiled (and ignored Saff). "Oh, come here," she giggled, and hugged Liam again, and this time she didn't let go for ages and ages.

When Liam went, we had a few games of cards, and then watched *Embarrassing Bodies* on the ancient TV on the kitchen counter (and decided that, actually, things *could* be worse – we could all have raging red boils on our bums!). Then we went off for early nights.

I woke up about two o'clock with the spiny bits in the mattress digging into me and realized that Mum wasn't there. Knowing that the flat was now rat-free and so it was safe to get out of bed for some water, I headed for the kitchen.

I found her sitting at the table. She'd taken her engagement ring off and was staring at it, like she was going to tell someone's fortune.

I wasn't sure whether to go in or not – I thought maybe she just wanted to be alone. But then she glanced over and said, "Hi."

"Hi. Drink?" I asked, reaching for a glass.

She shook her head. "You know, I really thought my marriage would last for ever," she said, as I turned on the tap. She laughed, but not in a good way. "Well, I don't suppose *anyone* gets married thinking they're going to split up. But still, I feel like such an idiot."

I turned round and leaned against the sink. "You're not. Dad is."

She shrugged. "I was lying in bed just now, racking my brains, trying to remember whether I'd packed anything valuable that we could sell, just to pay this blessed rent and keep a roof over our heads. I can't believe I didn't think about money when we left Ealing. There was my whole jewellery box – I could have sold the really good pieces and sent the rest to one of those 'We Buy Gold' places. And my scarves – the one I was wearing is on the sofa, but I could have shoved the others in my bag. That would have been another thousand pounds right there, even just selling them on eBay. And those little delft figurines in the front living room… Goodness only knows how much…" She sighed. "Oh well, it's all gone now. I just thought of grabbing things like underwear and our toothbrushes! How hopeless! How can I expect to start a business thinking like that?"

"But no one can run a business without clean knickers on," I said, trying to make her smile.

She did, for a moment anyway. "Then I realized… my ring," she said. "It would pay our rent for the next few months and set the beauty parlour in motion."

I felt my heart quicken. Was she serious?

"But Mum, would you really want to sell it?" I asked.

She spun it on the table. "I don't know. Urgh! It means so much to me, and at the same time I'm so angry with your dad that I never want to see the bloody thing again! Every time I look at it, it just reminds me of the hopes and dreams we had, and how they've all been shattered. But then, it also makes me remember that we *did* have so many happy times too. I thought your dad and I would still be chatting and laughing about them in our old age, but now I'm on my own."

I felt awful for her then. "You've got us," I said. "We'll always be here for you."

"Oh, Abbie, bless you, love," she said, her voice going wobbly. "And honestly I do know that even with what's happened, I'm still so, so lucky. I love you girls more than you'll ever know. I just wish I could stop feeling so angry all the time. Okay, so things weren't perfect between your dad and me, but marriages never are. Still, we had more than most people could wish for, and I don't mean money – I mean three wonderful daughters, good friends, a lovely home full of laughter and happiness. Why did he have to wreck it all?"

That gave me a start. For the first time, it struck me – our *home* was gone. Not just the house, but the *home*. I'd always assumed Mum and Dad would be there, together, and that I'd go back in the holidays from uni, and take my kids there, and have birthdays and Christmases there. But now…would they even be able to be in the same room as each other again? What about when one of us graduated or got married – would we have to leave Dad out?

I felt sick, realizing that it wasn't just the present that had gone, but the future as well. I desperately wished I could just wave a magic wand and make everything alright, but I couldn't.

"Oh, Abbie, I could brain that man!" Mum cried suddenly. "Why did he have to break everything? How could he do this to us?" Then she stopped just as suddenly and sighed. "I promised myself I wouldn't get into all this with you girls, especially not you, Abs. You're too young to deal with it. I'll end up making you all bitter and twisted."

I leaned over the back of her chair and put my arms round her shoulders. "I'm glad you're talking to me," I told her. "You know you always can. I'm not too young to understand."

Mum shook her head. "No. It's not on. I'm the mother. I should be asking you how *you're* doing. How *are* you doing?"

For a moment I thought about sharing my feelings with her. But I decided that she had enough problems to focus on, and besides, it felt like if I started talking about it I'd never stop. So I just said, "I'm fine, really."

"You always were the strong one, Abbie," Mum said then, and for some reason I felt as queasy as when Saff had said it, during our welly-throwing session after the car was taken. Mum picked up her engagement ring and held it in her palm. "It's time for me to be strong too. I know what to do with this now. We need to start again, and this ring could be the key to our future."

"You're selling it?"

She nodded and I felt a rush of relief. We weren't going to be out on the street — not this week anyway. And if she got a good price, well, maybe we had a shot at making my business idea work.

Then, with a lot of tugging and twisting, she took her wedding ring off too. "There's no point wearing this any more either. I'll keep it, though. One of you girls might want it one day."

I couldn't help laughing. "None of us even have boyfriends yet."

Mum smiled. "No rush on that score," she said. "The last thing I need right now is three hysterical lovesick teenagers rampaging round the flat."

"Don't worry. I can't see that scenario happening any time soon. Not in my case, anyway," I told her.

"Listen, don't say anything to Saff and Grace about the ring, will you, till I've done it?" Mum said. "I don't want to get their hopes up about staying if I can't sell it before our delightful landlord gets back tomorrow."

I grinned at her. "My lips are sealed."

We had a big hug then and I said goodnight. And when I got back into bed, the sticky-out mattress bits didn't seem so bad, somehow.

Chapter Six

On Wednesday, Grace and I walked home together after school. Saff met up with us halfway and she was all buzzed up. She'd been on a new intake open day at the college and although she was nervous about whether she'd get a place (she was sure she hadn't passed *any* of her GSCEs), she was really excited too. She told us all about it as we walked back to the flat.

"I've made friends with this girl Emily who's applying too – we're meeting up in town tomorrow. And Sally, who teaches a lot of Level One, is really nice. I know I wasn't keen at first, but I think this course could be perfect for me after all. If I take the make-up option from Level Two onwards, we'll be doing TV and film and special effects and stuff. Or if I go down the massage route, in Level Three we get to do complementary therapies, like Indian Head Massage."

"Ewww!" squealed Grace. "How horrible! Rubbing someone's yucky head! That's about as gross as being a dentist or a podiatrist!"

"No it isn't!" Saff snapped. "And anyway, I'll give you dentist – I couldn't bear staring into people's mouths all day – but children? What's wrong with *them*?"

"Podiatrists are for *feet*, you idiot," Grace said haughtily. "Children is *paediatrician*."

"I *know* that," Saff said witheringly. "I *was* joking."

"Yeah right," Grace said, looking smug. "Anyway, get real, Saff. You're going on about Level Three but, in case you've forgotten, we probably won't even be here *next week*. We've got no money, remember? Our benefits are on their way but they'll be too late. We're getting kicked out on the street *tonight* and goodness knows where we'll end up."

Saff looked wide-eyed at Grace like she actually *had* forgotten. It was amazing how she seemed to be able to switch things on and off in her head, just like that. I bit my lip. I knew I'd promised Mum not to say anything about our chat the night before, but Saff looked so scared…

My sisters were completely deflated as we reached the flat, and as we trooped up the stairs I vowed to make Mum tell them about selling the ring, the minute we got in. But I didn't have to, because we walked into the kitchen and…

"Woah!" they gasped at once.

Mum was sitting at the table behind a huge pile of cash and, weirdly, a plate of carefully arranged Viscount biscuits.

"Oh my God, did you rob a bank?" Saff cried. "There's, like, a million quid there."

Grace gave her a withering look and was just about to speak when Mum said, "Nine and a half thousand actually. I could have got more but I didn't have much bargaining power because I needed the money on the spot."

"But how…?" Grace began.

"I sold my engagement ring," said Mum.

"Mum!" Grace shrieked. "That's supposed to be a family heirloom! And anyway, what were you thinking, walking round town with that kind of cash on you? You could have been mugged!"

"Grace, calm down!" Mum cried. "Liam was here doing the skirting board and he drove me to the jeweller's. I'm glad I had him with me too, because they were only offering eight thousand to start with and he talked them up."

Meanwhile, the wheels in Saff's brain had been turning. "Yes! Get in!" she whooped suddenly. "Now we're loaded, I can still go up to London for my singing lessons, and get a whole new wardrobe, and—"

"We are *not* loaded," Mum said firmly. "This is for our *rent*." Then she smiled, and winked at me. "And our new business."

I absolutely screamed then. "Really? We've got enough money?" I shrieked.

Mum nodded. "Just."

I threw myself at her and hugged her tight. "That's amazing! Oh, that's fantastic!" I felt in shock, like I couldn't take it in.

Grace and Saff gaped at her. "Seriously?" Grace gasped.

"We're actually doing it?" cried Saff.

Mum grinned. "Yep. We'll have to be really, really strict with the budget, though." She slapped Saff's hand away from the biscuit plate. "And don't touch those, they're for Mr. Vulmer."

"What?" Grace snarled. "We can't let that man in here, not after how threatening he was to us last week! We should have called the police!"

Mum grimaced. "Oh, come on, Grace, that's a bit overdramatic," she said. "He didn't threaten us, and it's true we haven't paid him a penny as yet, so I'm not surprised he's annoyed. But, in case you've forgotten, we need to rent the shop downstairs from him to make any of this happen. It'll take a major charm offensive to get him to agree to let us have it with our tiny budget, so that's what we're going to do."

Mum glanced at her watch and leaped up. "Oh goodness, we've only got ten minutes. Quick, give me a hand to tidy up."

I did say that trying to tidy up was a bit pointless because the flat actually looked better with our stuff strewn around it, covering up the grossness. But Mum gave me such an exasperated look that I picked up our bags and the growing pile of recycling on the kitchen counter and shoved it all in the bathroom.

The doorbell rang and then there was the scratching of a key in the lock. Mum took a deep breath and smoothed down her blouse and skirt. "Remember, girls – charm offensive," she said sternly and then swished off into the hallway.

"Do come in," we heard her say in her poshest voice.

"I will, seeing as it's my flat," Mr. Vulmer replied gruffly, wheezing his way up the hall and into the kitchen. We all stood in a line by the table, smiling, trying not to look alarmed by the scarily-bright palm-tree-patterned shirt he was wearing. We said a cheery "hello" in unison, but Mr. Vulmer ignored us. He'd clocked the pile of bank notes on the table, though. We'd put most of it away, for the business (well, fingers crossed), but the rest sat enticingly in front of him.

"Do sit down," said Mum. "The kettle's on."

Mr. Vulmer sneered. "I'm not stopping. I'm just here to collect my money." He reached out for the cash but Mum moved it to one side and offered him the plate instead. "Biscuit?" she offered, with a stuck-on smile. "You look like a Viscount man to me. You know, classy."

Mr. Vulmer peered at her suspiciously. "I prefer a digestive actually. I can't be doing with fiddly wrappers."

"You could do with staying off *all* biscuits or you'll be heading for a heart attack," Saff advised.

Oh dear. When Mum said "charm offensive", Saff seemed to have only heard the "offensive" part.

Luckily, Mum sent her down to the shop sharpish for some digestives, and then started telling Mr.

Vulmer about how much we liked the flat, now we'd got used to it, and how well Grace and I had settled in at school here. She also went on about what a wonderful town it was, as though Mr. Vulmer was personally responsible for the gorgeous old buildings, quirky little shops and beautiful open spaces of Totnes. Then she broached the subject of our business idea

Usually, Mum can charm anyone – traffic wardens, waiters, shop assistants, you name it – but it wasn't working on our landlord. And when she said we could only give him a hundred a week for the flat and fifty to rent the shop unit, he actually *snorted* in disbelief. "That's a prime retail space – I could ask two-fifty a week!" he wheezed. "And as for the flat, we said one-fifty. It's not up for negotiation."

I really started to worry then, and Mum looked panicked too. If *she* couldn't persuade him, what hope did the rest of us have?

But there was one force we hadn't reckoned on: Grace. She'd been silent the entire time, and I thought she'd just been sulking about the whole calling-the-police thing. But no. She'd been listening to every word, and thinking, and now she struck.

She fixed him with an intense stare. "I know you're a shrewd man, Mr. Vulmer," she began. "A man of

119

business. A man of property. A man who is not going to be sweet-talked by biscuits. Not even digestives."

"Oh, what?" cried Saff, as she walked back in, biscuit packet in hand. "So I went all that way for no reason?"

Grace shot her a *shut up* look and returned her attention to Mr. Vulmer. "The fact that so far you have been uninterested in our offer...well, we obviously haven't explained the proposition clearly enough, which is our fault and we apologize. If we had, a man as astute as yourself would have given it more consideration." She leaned forward across the table and fixed him with an intense look. "You say you could rent the shop unit out for two hundred and fifty a week, and yet it's obviously been empty for a long time."

He shrugged. "Yeah, well, hard times, innit?"

"By accepting our offer, you'll be getting security for your property against vandalism, and safety from squatters whom, as I'm sure you're aware, can take months and thousands in legal fees to get rid of."

He snorted again. "You lot *are* the bloomin' squatters. I just want my rent, that's all, or you'll be out on the street. Today."

Mum and Saff flinched at that, and I felt my

stomach flip over, but Grace continued without a flicker of emotion. "Not to mention keeping the place warm, so it won't fall down with damp or crumble away with dry rot. The shop fit will add thousands in value to *your* property and we're not asking you for a penny towards it. It's a no-risk situation. You could have both the shop and this flat secure, with no hassle at all and almost two grand in your pocket, as payment up front for the next three months. Cash." She picked up the wodge of money and wafted it in his face. He stared at it, like a snake being charmed. She raised her eyebrows and smiled. "Frankly, Mr. Vulmer, *you* should be paying *us*."

Saff's forehead wrinkled in confusion. "Well, hang on, why isn't he then?"

Grace shot her another *shut up* look and fanned herself with the bank notes, trying to look nonchalant. We all waited, hardly daring to breathe.

"Fine, okay, deal," he said gruffly.

Grace shouted "Yes!", then composed herself and added, "I'm so pleased we could come to an agreement." Mr. Vulmer reached for the money but she drew it back. "There must be contracts first, of course," she said imperiously. "I'll get a standard Assured Shorthold Tenancy agreement off the net for the flat, and find out what we need for the shop."

For a second it looked like he was going to argue, but he was defenceless against the force of Grace Green.

"And if you could just pop the keys for the shop over later that would be great," Mum said, stepping in again. "We need to get in and look at the state of everything, so we can start planning the refit."

"I've got them here," he said, rummaging in his pocket and dropping the keys into Mum's hand. She looked at them in disbelief, lying in her palm just as her ring had been last night – as if she'd magically transformed one into the other.

"Excellent," said Grace, taking over again. "Mum, *and Liam*," she added pointedly, "can drop the contracts in to you tomorrow and settle up. Nice doing business with you."

"And you, ladies," grunted Mr. Vulmer. He reached for the digestives but Saff whipped the packet away and Grace bustled him out the door. Mum and I just stood there, staring at each other and grinning.

As soon as my sisters came back in we all hit the roof with excitement, jumping round the kitchen in a huddle and screaming, "YEEEEEEEEEEES!"

Grace was absolutely glowing as we all went on about how amazing she'd been. We got into complete hysterics when Saff whipped off Grace's glasses, put them on and did an impression of her leaning across the table and saying, "Frankly, Mr. Vulmer, *you* should be paying *us*."

"I can't believe it!" gasped Mum, when we'd finally got our breath back.

"We're really doing it!" I cried. "It was just an idea, but now it's going to be real. We're actually creating our own business! We're making our dreams come true!"

I could see it in my mind: the gorgeous treatment rooms, thick soft towels, vases of bright flowers. I could hear the relaxing music…smell the luxurious fresh face masks and body creams…taste the delicious juices and smoothies…

Five minutes later, we were all stood under the single fizzling light bulb in the filthy, dingy shop unit. It felt less like we were making our dreams come true and more like we'd made the worst mistake of our lives.

Mum picked her way through the broken dust-covered desks and swivel chairs that filled our reception/shop/smoothie bar to remove a faded (and, as Grace pointed out, extremely sexist) calendar from the wall. The torn, yellowed posters of people with perms and big shoulder pads sipping cocktails on exotic balconies told us that it had once been a travel agency. Our gorgeous luxury treatment rooms were two vile back offices with curled-up brochures strewn all over the stained, fuzzy carpet and striped eighties paper peeling off the walls. The little kitchen was beyond unhygienic and as for the loo…urgh, I didn't even want to *think* about it.

I mean, we'd known it would need work, but *this* much work? I started to wonder whether Mr. Vulmer *had* got the better deal after all. Were we mad, taking this on? How could we possibly transform somewhere so disgusting into the luxurious haven of tranquillity and relaxation I had in my mind? How could somewhere so dull, drab and dusty ever become the beauty parlour we dreamed of?

I knew we were all having similar wobbles because when Mum said, "Yes, well, I think we've seen enough for the moment," no one argued. In fact, we couldn't get back up to the flat fast enough (and *that's* saying something!).

But back upstairs the shock wore off and the excitement shone through again as we began making plans for the business. The seven and a half grand we had left after paying out the two rents seemed like a huge amount of money at first, but Mum was right, once we started thinking about all the stuff we needed, it suddenly didn't seem like very much at all.

We worked out that, for the reception area, we'd need a desk and chair, a till, nice sofas, some kind of worktop to make the smoothie bar, and stools for people to sit at it, a manicure station, shelving for the products we were going to sell, and nice bags to put them in. Oh, and an appointments book – until we could afford a computer, anyway.

"The treatment rooms will need massage tables," said Mum, "foot spas for the luxury pedicures, chests of drawers, towels, heaters, hairbands, clocks, dressing gowns, a music system…"

Grace frowned. "That sounds expensive."

Mum nodded. "Yes, well, when I say a music system, I'm probably talking about a couple of second-hand CD players… Oh, and we'll need stuff for waxing."

Grace and Saff dissolved into giggles at that.

"What?" Mum cried. "Most beauty places offer that service, and I'm qualified in it, so why not?"

"Rather you than me, that's all I can say!" squealed Saff.

Grace shuddered. "There's no way I'm ripping off someone's leg hair, or *worse*!"

When we'd all stopped giggling, and Mum had stopped rolling her eyes, we got back on with the list.

In the loo (urgh!), at least the plumbing was there, which Mum said would save us heaps of money, but we all agreed we'd have to make it a LOT nicer before it was fit for paying customers. And we'd need a small staff area for keeping cleaning equipment and stock (the kitchenette that was there would do, but the same applied as with the loo!).

We also wrote down: paint for EVERYWHERE! Plus a stock of trade products that I couldn't make, like the nail varnishes, nail files and organic wax. And money for a two-day Manicure Diploma for Saff, so she could help Mum with clients right away, without waiting for her college course to begin. Then we needed ingredients for our home-made products, plus jars and labels, pans, measuring jugs, spoons, moulds and things. I'd got enough glycerine soap base and sweet almond, olive and grapeseed oils left to make some products for the photo shoot I was planning to do with Summer (once I'd asked her, of course!) but for the actual shop stock we'd have to buy loads more.

"Nice plants and pictures," Saff added then.

"Phone line and actual phone, more *importantly*," said Grace sniffily.

"Finishing touches *are* important," Saff argued. "They're what make the place look inviting."

"I'm just saying, it's lucky I'm here to think of the essentials," Grace shot back. "No phone equals no bookings equals no customers equals no money."

As my sisters bickered, Mum was staring in alarm at the list, which was running into its third page. "Oh dear, we really haven't got *anything*, have we?" she muttered, frowning. "And from what I remember from the beauty place I used to work in, we still need to allow for product testing by a cosmetic chemist. Then there are smoke alarms and extinguishers, an electrical check and safety certificate, and anything else that comes up in our health and safety inspection…"

"Don't forget a proper pest control assessment by Rentokil and any treatment," added Saff, with a shudder. "I don't think the health and safety people are going to accept Liam's 'cheese, spade and running round screaming' method."

Mum looked anxiously at Grace, who had been roughly estimating the costs and allocating a budget to each thing as we went along. "Do you think we can even *do* this?" she asked anxiously.

Grace frowned at the figures, then said, "We need to keep the range of products fairly small to begin with, with simple ingredients, and look for bargains, and ask for good deals wherever we can. But…yes, I think so."

"We're in business!" Saff cried.

Mum and I shared a smile. It wasn't going to be easy, but it was really happening.

"Just one thing," Mum said then. "What are we going to call it?"

All three of them looked at me, expecting me to come out with something on the spot. For a moment my mind was blank, but then I thought about how we weren't just chasing rainbows, and then of that song "Somewhere Over The Rainbow", and then about dreams coming true and… "How about Rainbow Beauty?" I said.

"Perfect," Mum declared, and Grace and Saff agreed it was the right name too, without arguing for once.

I'd like to say that we toasted our new idea – business, adventure, dream – in champagne, or at least in the luxury fruit smoothies we used to whizz up using every tropical fruit under the sun. But for now, orange squash would have to do.

"It's a good job Liam fancies you, Mum," Grace said grumpily. "We'd never be able to afford full price for a shop fit." Then she just stared at us all as we collapsed into fits of giggles. "What?" she demanded.

"Oh, honey," Mum gasped, "you're so, so clever, but you can't see what's right under your nose!"

"Liam's gay – how could you not notice?" said Saff, creasing up again.

So then as Grace harrumphed around the kitchen, demanding to know when Liam had actually *said* that, and Saff offered to paint Mum's nails to practise for her practical interview at the college, I couldn't help smiling to myself. For the first time since we'd got here, we felt like *us*.

I could almost pretend that we were still in our lovely house in Ealing, and that Dad was just about to walk in the door.

Chapter Seven

I couldn't wait to get to school on Thursday morning. Summer and Ben were in our form room already, sitting on their desks, and I launched myself at them and pulled them both into a hug.

"Erk!" cried Summer.

"Steady on, Abs," gasped Ben. "Is this how you plan to make some money, becoming a wrestling champion?"

Well, okay, I was so excited it *was* probably more of a headlock than a hug. "We're staying!" I announced gleefully, as I put them down. "We got the rent – Mum sold her engagement ring. And I had an idea for a business – a beauty parlour in the shop downstairs from our flat. Our landlord's going to let it to us, and our neighbour Liam's going to help us fit the place out – he's a builder – and I'm going to make all the products myself, and Mum will do the treatments and—"

"That's fantastic!" cried Summer, getting *me* into a headlock then.

"Yeah, brilliant!" added Ben, throwing himself in too. We started whooping and jumping up and down in a huddle.

Then I heard, "Hey y'all. Why the love-in?"

It was Marco.

I stopped jumping, untangled myself from Summer and Ben, and beamed at him. "I'm staying," I said.

His face broke into a massive smile. "Oh, Abbie, that's great." He looked awkward for a moment, like he didn't know what to do next.

"Well hug her, you idiot," cried Summer.

I felt awkward too (as you know, hugging someone you've got a bone-shaking knee-wobbling crush on isn't the same as hugging your mates). But we hugged, and it went on for ages and ages, as I couldn't make myself let go, and Marco didn't seem in a hurry to end it either.

"Erm, are you going for a record or something..."

said Ben, making me blush bright red and finally prise myself away from Marco. Luckily I got into telling them all the details about Rainbow Beauty then, so the World's Longest Hug cringe faded after a while (and so did my cheeks!).

Summer said that of course we could do a promotional leaflet for our Media project, and when I mentioned about the juices and smoothies, she insisted that we could have loads of fruit and veg from their garden. How amazing is that? I told her we'd pay for it, of course, but she wouldn't hear of it. She even said she'd sow a few more rows of carrot seeds in their veggie patch for me, so by September we should have loads of those for the juices. And Ben reckons that by then people have so many apples they put boxes of them by the side of the road and you can just take them, for free. He said we could go round collecting them, and that he'd show me how to store them so they'd last the whole winter.

"I've got no idea about fruit and veg," said Marco then, "or skin creams and that, but I'll help in any way I can."

It was so sweet of him, I felt like hugging him again, but I managed to resist, because otherwise I probably wouldn't have been able to let go of him *ever*, whatever jokes Ben made!

When Grace and I got home, I was absolutely buzzing, and I told Mum and Saff all about my friends' offers of help. They were grimy but happy after spending the day trying to clean up the shop, and the news made them even bubblier.

"I met Emily in town earlier," Saff told me and Grace, "and she said she'll help too, when we open, with manicures and that, or tidying up and making tea. It'll be good experience for when our course starts."

"Oh, that's fab," I cried. "And with Liam too, we're getting a proper team together!"

"That's great," said Grace.

"I bet your mates are happy you're staying," I said to her. "I hope they're handy with a paintbrush!"

"Yeah, they are," she said shortly, then hurried up to the flat to start her homework. Hmm, getting info out of Grace was like getting blood out of a stone.

Anyway, I went after her, and as she got on with her maths project at the kitchen table, I started writing lists of the ingredients we needed to order from my supplier catalogues (which luckily I'd brought with me) and of the equipment we needed to buy ready to make our first batch of products. I had a few things, of course, and I'd been using stuff from the kitchen. But to make products to sell, everything had to be just kept specially for that, so we needed loads of new things too.

When I'd finished my draft list, Grace took it and interrogated me about whether we needed four mixing bowls and measuring jugs to start off with, or if we could manage with two, and whether some of the more expensive oils were really necessary. I managed to cross a few things off that I didn't think would affect the final products or slow down the production process too much, and finally she approved the list and let me ring the supplier on Mum's pay-as-you-go phone, so long as I promised to ask for a discount.

But even when I was actually ordering everything – the essential oils, bath foam, milk and lotion bases, flower petals and lavender buds, cute heart and star moulds for soaps, gauze bags, bottles, jars and ribbons, spatulas and stirrers – I could still hardly believe it was really happening.

My official timetable on Friday was Maths, English, double Geography and double Science after lunch, but really it should have said *Flirting, Flirting, double Flirting, break for lunch as Marco had band practice, more double Flirting*. Marco and I had to work together in

Maths, and his leg was accidentally leaning on mine under the desk. My brain was totally scrambled, thinking, *Is it really accidental? Or on purpose? Or accidental at first but now on purpose?* My heart was pounding and I could hardly breathe, let alone *calculate* anything, so he had to do most of the work.

Then in Geography we got into a pretend-scrap over a pencil sharpener and Mrs. Leavis said, "Marco, put Abbie down and get on with your work," really loudly, and *everyone* turned round to look at us. I nearly *died* of embarrassment, while feeling really excited at the same time. I mean, if a teacher had noticed, surely that meant there must be something *to* notice, didn't it?!

It's not like I'd forgotten what Summer and Ben had said about Marco. But it was different with me and him. I just knew it.

On Saturday morning I went to the greengrocer's with a long list of fruit and veg, plus strict instructions from Grace to get as much money off as possible. The plan was to put everything out on the kitchen table and have a go at making some different juice blends to see which worked. There were things we were definitely going to use, like apples and carrots as bases for most of the juices, but apart from that it was a case of experimenting. I knew I wanted to use oranges and lemons though, so that we could express the oil from the peel to scent our orange and lemon soaps, and set them with strips of peel in so they looked really cool.

I was there to buy ingredients for my fresh face masks too. I'd been keen to do an anti-aging one with asparagus and kiwi fruit, but Grace had vetoed that, because as soon as asparagus is out of season it's going to be really expensive and kiwi fruit are about thirty pence each all the time. Luckily she agreed to blueberries because we can use them in the juices too, and we should hopefully be able to get a good deal for buying a lot. I say luckily because the night before, while trying to avoid the spiny bits in bed again, I'd come up with the idea of having one juice for each colour of the rainbow, and blueberries are the only way of making blue juice. Plus they're super foods, full of antioxidants, so they give a great burst of nutrients as well as being scrummy. I also had to get limes, strawberries, peaches, pears, ginger, grapes, pineapples, spinach, beetroot, melon, passion fruits, mangoes and bananas.

It was really cool in the greengrocer's. They had loads of organic and fair trade products, and thankfully not at crazy high prices. The whole place was decked out with retro advertising signs and old orange crates, and they had these lovely old weighing scales too. I was really nervous at first about talking to the greengrocer (called Tom, as I found out), especially as I had to ask for a discount (yikes!). But it was fine in the end – I said how nice the shop looked and we just got chatting.

As we were talking I had the brainwave that it would be great to use the grocer's as the location for the photo shoot Summer and I were planning for our promotional leaflet. I explained about starting up Rainbow Beauty and asked if we could, and Tom was really keen. That's when I decided it would be a good moment to ask for a discount. Amazingly, he said that as we'll be buying a lot of fruit and veg, I could have ten per cent off everything! I could have hugged him, but I didn't because then Ben walked in with his mum and his baby bro.

"Oh, hi," he mumbled, looking really interested in his baseball boots.

"Hi," I replied, wondering why he was shuffling awkwardly.

Ben's mum gave me a big smile, and so did the gorgeous baby. "Well, aren't you going to introduce us?" she prompted.

"This is Abbie," Ben mumbled.

"Oh!" his mum cried. "So *you're* the famous Abbie! Ben hasn't stopped talking about you since you started at Cavendish. Abbie this, Abbie that. Abbie, Abbie, Abbie."

"Oh my God, Mum!" he cried.

So that's why he was looking so awkward. He was on Embarrassing Parent Alert. I raised my eyebrows at him teasingly, expecting him to pull a face back or something. But can you believe it, he actually *blushed*. "Come on, let's go," he mumbled. "We can live without fruit and veg this week."

But his mum just smiled at me again. "I'm Trina. This is Gabe."

"Hi, nice to meet you," I said, then leaned down to little Gabe in his buggy. "And *you*, gorgeous little man. You are gorgeous, aren't you? You are!"

Gabe wriggled and cackled with delight. Then I started beeping his nose and making him laugh even more.

"Right, well, I'm going to—" Ben began, heading for the door.

"No, you stay and give Abbie a hand," Trina said, eyeing my two huge half-filled boxes. "She can't carry both of those on her own."

Ben gave her an exasperated look but she just

smiled sweetly at him and said, "Don't worry, I'm not going to cramp your style for much longer. I'll just get our things and be on my way. I'll see you at home."

When she'd bought their shopping and I'd fussed over Gabe a bit more, we said goodbye to them (well, I did – Ben just grunted). He started to look a bit more of a normal colour then.

"I'm so sorry about her," he said, wincing. "I don't go on about you, honestly. I've barely mentioned you."

"Oh, right. Well, *thanks*," I teased.

He grinned. "No, I mean, she's only trying to embarrass me."

"And she's *brilliant* at it," I said. "Look, thanks for staying. I hadn't even thought about how to get this lot back to the flat."

"No worries. What's next?" he asked.

I looked down the list. "Six mangoes. And make sure you only pick the heaviest ones, they're the juiciest, and give them a little squeeze with your thumb first to make sure they're ripe." With the amount of smoothies we'd had in our Ealing house, I knew what a big difference it made to start off with the best ingredients.

Ben saluted. "Yes, boss."

"Don't be cheeky. Here, catch." I threw a pineapple to him. Okay, well maybe a little bit *at* him.

"Oi, careful!" he cried, as he caught it and put it in the box. "You could have had my eye out with that thing!"

When we'd got everything, I settled up with Tom and arranged to come the following day after school to do the photo shoot. Then Ben and I picked up the boxes and headed for the flat. He insisted on taking the heaviest one but still, my arms were killing me by the time we got to the main door. Balancing the box on my knee, I unlocked it and we trudged up the stairs. I'd thought I might mind him seeing the flat, but now that he was there it didn't bother me. I *was* worried about Saff and Grace, though. "It's only fair to warn you, my sisters can be a bit over the top," I told him as I let us in.

I was glad I did warn him in advance because of course Saff and Grace were hideously embarrassing. It was even worse than I thought because Mum wasn't there to keep a lid on them. She'd gone to Argos and Poundland in Torquay with Liam to get all the kitchen equipment we needed for making the products, like the measuring jugs and pans and spoons and things. Of course, I'd ordered the moulds and most of the base ingredients and oils from my usual specialist supplier (and they'd arrived in a big box that morning, luckily), but we were buying anything we could in cheaper places.

"Oooooh, you've got *him* well trained," said Saff from the sofa, as we walked into the kitchen and dumped the boxes on the floor.

"You shouldn't get a man to do your lifting and carrying for you, it's anti-feminist," Grace lectured.

"It's not cos he's a man…boy," I said, "but cos he's a *person*, with *hands*. I didn't see either of *you* offering to help. Anyway, what happened to 'hi' and 'nice to meet you'?"

"Hi and nice to meet you," they chanted together, and burst into giggles.

"Hi," Ben mumbled, then stood there looking about as embarrassed as when his mum had started the whole Famous Abbie thing. He obviously decided he'd suffered enough for one day, because he mumbled an excuse about getting back to help out with Gabe's lunch and made a sharp exit.

"That was Ben, one of my new mates that I told you about, not that he'll dare come round here again," I snapped. "Thanks for making him feel so welcome! Why couldn't you just be nice like normal people?"

Grace rolled her eyes, and Saff went, "Oooohhh! Don't get your knickers in a twist, sis! Fancy him, do you?"

"No, actually," I huffed. "If you must know, I'm into someone else."

Saff was all ears then and even Grace looked up from her costings spreadsheet, but I did the zipping-my-lips sign. "Dream on! As if I'd tell you *anything* after that performance!"

"Ooooh, sorry, miss!" Saff teased.

"Right, let's get this table cleared and set all the stuff out," I said, ignoring her. "As soon as Mum gets back we need to start sorting out the smoothies and getting these products done." When neither of them moved I gave them death stares and started clearing the table myself. Among the debris, there was an open letter to Saff from the college. "Oh, you've got your interview next Wednesday – why didn't you say?" I asked her.

"It's no big deal," she said, trying to sound casual. "Even if I do okay in it, and the practical assessment, they won't be able to tell me for sure if I'm in until I get my GCSE results."

"Oh, Saff, you mustn't worry about—" I began but Grace cut in. "How many GCSEs do you *need* to file someone's nails, anyway?" she said snottily.

"There's much more to it than that!" Saff snapped back. "I told you, the course includes massage and make-up, and I can take a business module alongside it too so I can help make Rainbow Beauty a success."

Grace sat back in her chair and folded her arms. "Hang on, isn't this the course you said was rubbish?" she asked.

"Well, I was wrong about that. It's...I—" Saff looked completely exasperated, like she could cheerfully strangle Grace, and to be honest I felt like helping her. It was so obvious she really wanted to get into college now, and that she was terrified her grades would let her down.

"Lay off her, Grace," I warned. Then I said to Saff, "Wait and see, perhaps you did better than you think in your exams. And even if you didn't, maybe they'll be a bit flexible if you show them how keen you are."

"Yeah, thanks, Abs," said Saff, giving Grace a wounded look. "I think I'll go and have a look at what I've got to wear for the interview."

"Typical," snorted Grace. "That's your first thought, what you're going to wear. It's not about how you *look*, Saff."

"Oh, just do one," said Saff, sticking her fingers up at Grace as she walked out of the kitchen.

As soon as she was out of earshot I turned on Grace. "Why are you being such a cow?" I demanded. "You know how much Saff wants to get on that course now. Why aren't you supporting her?"

Grace just shrugged. "She needs to be realistic, that's all. She made zero effort for her GCSEs and she still expects to get what she wants. It doesn't work like that."

I was just about to tell her I thought that was really harsh, but then Mum and Liam walked in the door, piled up with bags and boxes. My stomach flipped over with excitement at actually *seeing* all the stuff and I started opening the box of stainless steel saucepans straight away. "Right, I'll get these washed out—"

"Sterilized," Grace, self-appointed queen of the health and safety guidelines, corrected.

"Sterilized," I continued. "Grace, you can cut up the soap base and Mum—"

"That can wait until tomorrow," Liam said, with a mischievous look on his face. "After the week you've all had, you need some R & R. It's a gorgeous day and we're going to the beach."

Yes! I was so excited, and Mum and Saff were too. Grace grumbled that she still had all the product budgets to do, and a heap of forms to fill in for the cosmetic testing, so she couldn't possibly spare the time. But when it came down to it, she didn't want to be left in the flat on her own either, so she came with us, stuffing her sheets and files into her bag.

In the rush to leave Ealing, Mum, Grace and I had forgotten to pack our swimming costumes, but luckily Saff had grabbed about six bikinis from her drawer and shoved them into her case, so she shared them out between us. I bagsied the blue spotted one, and the top was a bit big on me – okay, a *lot* big – but it was better than nothing. (As in the phrase! Not that I would actually wear NOTHING!)

Luckily Liam's van was that kind with a small back seat before the actual storage bit, so we all managed to fit in, just about. Saff and Grace were still fighting so I made sure I sat in between them to keep the peace.

When we arrived and spilled out into the car park, I couldn't help smiling. It was wonderful – a strong sea breeze, the fresh ozone smell, the sun blazing down. It was like standing in a holiday postcard. There were some loos and a few food stands and that's when we realized it was lunchtime.

Grace seemed to have cheered up a bit, though I knew if anyone pointed that out she'd go all grumpy again. "I'm thinking fresh-made doughnuts," she said.

"I'm thinking fish and chips," said Saff.

"I'm thinking seaweed wraps," I muttered to myself, staring out at the low rocks covered in bladderwrack that dotted the beach.

"What?" Saff spluttered.

"Oh no! Not to eat!" I gasped, giggling. "I mean, we could make seaweed body masks and offer a full wrap treatment at Rainbow Beauty. I made a batch of them once before, remember, with that seaweed powder, and you all thought they were really good."

"Oh, yeah," said Saff. "Nice idea."

"And I could make up a clay mask too," I said then, thinking aloud, "if we can find a good organic supplier who's not too expensive. And, hey, I know – we could create a Rainbow Beauty signature one as well, with layers of delicious creams and oils and then a wrapping to really let it sink into the skin. Maybe with rose oil lengthened out with geranium, and we could add wheatgerm for dry skin—"

"Abbie!" Liam cried, grinning. "I bring you for a nice day out and you're seeing work everywhere!"

I smiled back. "I can't stop my mind from coming up with stuff. Anyway, it's not work, it's fun."

"You won't be saying that when you're hauling those filthy desks out of the shop!" said Grace, but she was smiling too, for a change.

146

We settled on fish and chips in the end, with doughnuts and steaming coffee in cardboard cups for afters. Mum and Liam sat on the shingles, Mum with her big silk scarf draped round her, over her bikini, so that she actually looked *more* dressed than she did in her clothes. Liam kept pointing out fit guys to her and she kept insisting she was off men for ever, and he was saying things to make her laugh, like, *Oh goodie, more for me, then*.

Saff immediately stripped down to her bikini, slathered herself in sun cream and began to read her magazine, pretending not to notice all the boys deliberately walking past so they could check her out.

And Grace and I went swimming in the sea. It was exactly what I needed – the cold briny water really cleared my head (and washed off my make-up so it didn't look like I *had* a head, but never mind). As I floated on my back, rocked by the waves, watching the sun shimmering on the water, I felt happiness flood into me for the first time since all this happened. I had a nice school and lovely friends, our rent was paid up and our business was getting under way. Maybe this new life could really work out for us.

But then I felt instantly guilty for even thinking that. I mean, what about Dad? We hadn't spoken to him for almost a month. He didn't have Mum's new number and we had no way to contact him. I knew his mobile would have been cut off too, the same as ours. He was probably stuck in a dodgy B&B somewhere, or sleeping on a mate's sofa, with no money, no job and no family around him. Us four had each other, but he had no one.

Suddenly it felt like we were the ones who'd abandoned *him*, not the other way round. But I knew I couldn't say that to Mum or my sisters. They'd go mad — he was the bad guy, after all. And anyway, when I thought about what he'd done, I stopped feeling sorry for him and started feeling angry again. We *deserved* a fresh, new start after all the pain he'd put us through, and I was going to do everything I could to make sure we got one.

Chapter Eight

On Sunday morning we got to work creating our range of beauty products, juices and smoothies. We'd settled on holding a grand opening, with free samples, canapés, juices and mini-treatments, in two weeks' time (which Liam said was possible, just!). That would coincide with the beginning of the summer holidays, so that Grace and I could be there too, to look after reception, make the smoothies and keep things clean and tidy.

Mum had bought a surprise for us – pink-striped aprons like we had when we were little (but from the pound shop, not Whisk, this time!). It was strange, thinking that the last time we were all together wearing aprons like this and making yummy beauty stuff, I was sitting on the counter, the smallest little girl, being given the easy jobs and not allowed near the stove. And now I was in charge, directing everyone.

First we started on some little soaps. It was strange, scrubbing our hands and arms right up to the elbow, putting on hairnets (which we had hysterics over!) and sterilizing all the equipment before we started. It really made it feel like a proper professional business.

The scale was different too – instead of making, say, ten little star soaps, we were doing fifty. And where I sometimes guessed quantities, now I was having to weigh and measure everything out carefully, to make sure we stuck to the budget for each product. As Grace (aka the new Alan Sugar!) told me sternly, there was no point in making things that cost more to produce than we could sell them for. The other thing that soon became clear was that, if we were going to have any chance of getting as much as we hoped done before midnight, we'd have to work as a team. We weren't doing all the products in one day, of course. But we planned to make a good selection, and then we could add to that later in the week if we had time, as well as making up all the fresh face masks at the last minute. The masks only had about a three-week shelf life in the fridge, so we wanted to leave them as late as possible.

I set Saff to work on a couple of oranges and lemons with a grater, to get the strips of peel I wanted to put in the soaps, and Grace was in charge of squeezing the oil out of their skins, to give the soaps a really fresh, zesty smell. I melted the soap base myself because you have to be careful to get the temperature right or it goes all cloudy and brown, and then I added the orange or lemon oil. Mum was in charge of pouring the liquid soap into my cute little star moulds and adding a few strips of peel to each one before leaving them to set.

It seemed to take ages to do those, but we soon got into our stride and started turning out batches of Rose & Geranium Bath Bombs, and then lavender ones, which we named Luscious Lavender. Next we made a huge pan of Peppermint Kiss Lip Balm, which we tinted pink with alkanet root and put into the sweet coloured-glass pots I'd ordered, to set.

After a quick sandwich lunch, Mum and I tackled the Zingy Lemon Zest Foot Scrub, the Olive Grain Scrub and the Grapefruit Foot Lotion, and I let my sisters loose on the body butters. Grace was in charge of the avocado and mandarin varieties, while Saff did the cocoa butter and olive ones. For once, they just got on with it and didn't start arguing. Saff even managed to say that Grace's mandarin one smelled really scrummy, and Grace let her try some. The finished butters looked beautiful in their little pots, with the handmade labels in my swirly writing stuck onto their lids.

We finished off by inventing some bubble baths, and when they were all done we came up with names for the gorgeous yellow, purple and pink liquids in their tall, stoppered bottles – Zesty Zing, Lovely Lavender and Spicy Delight. Saff tied ribbons round their necks and attached pretty silver star decorations, while Grace cut out little card labels to tie on too. I wrote the names on the cards, and added *Handmade With Love by Rainbow Beauty* on each. We even came up with a slogan to put on our leaflets while we were working: *Rainbow Beauty – beauty from the inside out*. Nice, huh?

Then, later in the afternoon, seeing as everything was going so well (and we were really thirsty by then), we made a start on the juices. On the way back from the beach, I'd got Liam to pull up by a field so I could collect a big pile of nettles. They aren't at all yucky like you'd think – they don't sting your tongue (though I had to borrow his builders' gloves to pick them!), they're super immune-boosting and, best of all, they're free! And using them would reduce the amount of spinach we'd need to put into our green juice, so we'd save money there too.

Mum was in charge of creating the red and yellow juices, Saff chose orange, and Grace took green, so that left me with purple and blue. After lots of peeling and chopping, Grace chasing Saff round the room with a nettle and then the two of them having a small scrap over who was next to use the juicer, we set our inventions out on the table.

Me, Mum and Saff each made a couple of versions of our juices, to find the best ones, but Grace had insisted that her green one was the perfect recipe and that she only needed to make one version because as soon as we tried it we'd love it.

We tried Mum's first, and they were all really yummy, but we chose the one with peach, pear, lemon and strawberry for the red juice and the one with grapes, pears, apples and pineapple for yellow. Then it was my turn, and they all said they liked my carrot, apple and beetroot one for purple, even though they hadn't expected to (actually, Saff said, "Erm, Abs…drinking beetroot? Have you lost your mind?!"). Grace said it was extra good because it balanced out the cost of me choosing lots of the more expensive ingredients for my blue one, which was a vitamin burst of blueberries, melon, passion fruit and mango.

We were all in hysterics when we tried Saff's first version of the orange one. I mean, urgh! Mum squealed and made a sucking-a-lemon face, Grace said it would be fine to use as a window cleaner and I managed to gasp, "Maybe you could tone down the lime and ginger a bit. Okay, a *lot*." Luckily her second attempt, with much more carrot and orange, was really tasty.

Then it was Grace's turn.

"Right, this recipe is deliberately designed to be full of immune-boosting vitamins and minerals," she said proudly. We all took a sip and, well, it was such a shock that I couldn't help coughing and spluttering, and nor could Mum. Honestly, it was so disgusting I thought my tongue might drop off. Predictably, drama queen Saff rushed across the room and spat it down the sink. "Erm, Grace," I managed to gasp, "how on earth did you get *that* taste from the ingredients we had?"

My sister was frowning now. "I added my own," she stuttered. "I was going by that chart we've got about which foods are full of which vitamins. I wanted to make something to cleanse the digestion, so I added some cabbage and leeks from the fridge as well, and didn't bother with the carrots and apples."

"Urgh, *cabbage* juice?" groaned Saff. "That explains why it smells so bad! It's like drinking liquid farts!"

"But the carrots and apples are what give it a sweet taste, love," giggled Mum. "You can't just leave them out."

"I do think maybe the leeks make it a bit acidic," I wheezed, thumping my burning chest.

"You got loads of vitamins in," cried Saff, "you just forgot to make it taste good!" With that, we collapsed into giggles.

All except Grace.

Instead she looked furious. "Oh, typical, all laugh at me!" she snapped. "Well, thanks very much!"

"Hey, come on now," Mum cried. "We were just having a bit of fun."

"Yeah, everyone cracked up about my juice and *I* didn't mind," said Saff. "Why do you have to take everything so seriously?"

That's when Grace lost it. I mean, properly lost it. "Well I'm sorry I'm not as creative as you lot!" she shouted. "It's not nice being the odd one out, you know! You three are in your cosy little world, coming up with ideas all the time, being so pretty and sparkly and making new friends just like *that*." She clicked her fingers. "Well, lucky you. But not all of us find everything so easy."

We all stared at her in shock.

"You'll make some friends soon, honey," said Mum gently.

"No I won't!" Grace yelled. "It's different for me. I can't just walk up to people and start talking like you lot can. It took me years of junior school to get close to Bella and Jayne, and now I've had to leave them behind. Everyone's got their own groups at Cavendish."

I suddenly realized how lucky I was to have made friends so quickly. And I felt terrible that I hadn't noticed Grace was struggling. "You can hang out with us," I offered. "You've met Ben, he's really nice, and you've talked to Summer at the gate, and Marco's cool." I felt my stomach flip over, just saying his name out loud.

I'd thought Grace would be happy about that but instead she just gave me one of her death stares. "Thanks for taking pity on me," she said sarkily, "but I don't need my little sister coming to my rescue. I don't need anyone. I don't like anyone at school anyway, and they don't like me, so I'm better off on my own!" And before any of us had a chance to speak, she stormed off to her and Saff's room and slammed the door.

Mum looked horrified. "Why didn't she tell us she was feeling like that?" she gasped. "I could have gone into school and had a word with her form teacher."

Saff grimaced. "That's probably *why* she didn't say anything. Then she'd look like even more of a loser."

"She's not a loser," I said automatically.

"*I* know that," said Saff, "but you have to admit, she doesn't exactly help herself. She judges people so quickly. She doesn't give them a chance."

I didn't say anything to that, but secretly I agreed with Saff. Mum went down the hall and tried to talk to Grace but she wouldn't open the door. Saff and I tried too, and it was awful, because we could hear her sobbing and sobbing, but she just kept telling us to go away. In the end Mum said, "Come on, let's give her some space." I could tell she was really worried, we all were – but what could we do?

It was only when Mum and Saff had popped over to Liam's to talk about the shop fit that Grace shuffled into the kitchen. I'd finished off the fresh face mask samples I'd wanted to try out by then and

I was washing up for the millionth time.

In silence she picked up the tea towel and started drying stuff for me. Her eyes were red raw and I felt really bad for her. I tried to give her a hug but she wouldn't let me, so we just did the dishes for a while. Then, "I'm sorry about before, Abs," she said in a whisper. "It was really nice of you to offer to hang out with me, but it made me feel like even more of a sad case than ever."

"Just because you're not as outgoing as us, that doesn't make you a sad case," I insisted. "You're so clever, and you really care about things, and people." Grace smiled a little at that, so I carried on. "It's fine if it takes you a while to make friends," I told her. "You don't want to go round with just anyone, do you? You'll find people you really get on with. You need a bit of time, that's all."

"Yeah, I suppose," said Grace, still looking deflated. "But, like I said, everyone's got their groups, and anyway, I don't fit in anywhere. That's not the only problem, though. I don't think the level of Maths is all that good, and we can't afford a tutor any more. How on earth am I going to get into Cambridge at this rate?"

"Have you thought about telling your Maths teacher your ambition?" I asked. "It's Mr. Hayes, isn't it? I had him on Thursday when Mrs. Croft was ill. He seems quite nice. Maybe there's extension work you could do."

Grace smiled grimly. "Thanks for the idea, but everyone thinks I'm enough of a geek already, without me asking for extra work."

I felt suddenly protective. "Did someone *say* that to you?"

She sighed. "No, but I can tell that's what they're thinking. This girl Richanne and her lot look at me like I'm something they've found on the bottom of their shoes."

I tried to look upbeat, whilst vowing to find out who this Richanne was. "Well, if they think you're a geek already, you've got nothing to lose then, have you?" I countered. "Don't give up on your dreams, Gracie. Not because some girl looks at you funny. Not for anyone. After all we've been through, you can't let something like this drag you down."

She looked at me then, straight *at* me, and there was a new steel in her eyes. "Yeah, you're right," she said at last. "This is my whole future we're talking about, after all. Thanks, Abs."

"No problem," I said. "Now, can you please dry something else because you've been doing that cup for the last five minutes."

Grace looked down at the mug in her hands and giggled in surprise.

When Saff and Mum got back a few minutes later, Grace was waiting for them. "Saff, I'm sorry for not being very supportive about your interview," she said. "I really hope you get a place, and good enough grades to take it up."

"Thanks," Saff mumbled, with a small smile.

Mum gave Grace a hug even though she tried to struggle away. "Hon, you have to talk to me in future if you're upset," she said. "Please."

"I'm okay now," said Grace. She told them about our chat and what she'd decided about talking to her Maths teacher, and they both thought it was a good idea. Then Mum said, "Well done, Abbie, you've got the magic touch with your sisters, and me. We'd all have fallen apart by now if it wasn't for you."

I know she meant it nicely but it made me feel really sick, like when they keep going on about how strong I am, when actually, inside, I feel like shattering into bits half the time. So to change the subject I pushed a sample of fresh face mask across the table to each of them and said, "Right, get these on while I start on supper. There are three different versions to cover all the skin types, plus one relaxing and reviving with seaweed and aloe vera, and one soothing and cleansing with fresh blueberries and calamine. I need to know what you think… Besides, you're all looking a bit rough."

"Charming!" Mum cried and they all turned on me, protesting and jostling and giggling.

On Monday, I was in such a great mood because of all the beauty parlour stuff, and you know, *not* being chucked out on the street, that I was even more flirty with Marco than ever – which was what caused me to have a little mishap with the potassium chlorate in Science. We had to heat it up to melting point in a glass beaker and then (I found out later) carefully poke *one* gummy bear into it to see what happened. But I was so busy mucking about with Marco that I didn't hear the exact instructions (he was threatening to write *My heart sings with the joy of learning* on my exercise book, so I'd look like a total geek!). So I tipped half the little packet of Haribos into the beaker and it exploded with a massive whoosh and loads of steam came gushing out. I leaped about a metre into the air and screamed a word that made everyone turn round and stare at me *again* (CRINGE!). Even worse, Mr. Fellowes came and personally "helped" me with the next two experiments

(DOUBLE CRINGE!), i.e. he basically didn't let me touch *anything* apart from to wash up the beakers afterwards.

After school, Summer and I went to the greengrocer's to do the photo shoot for our leaflet. I still felt like pinching myself – I could hardly believe that we were there to get pictures of my own beauty products, for publicity about my family's new business.

The products looked so gorgeous in their little bottles and jars, with their handwritten labels. Tom, the greengrocer, let us have the complete run of the place, so first of all we arranged a big pile of oranges and lemons in one of the vintage orange crates and dotted the orange and lemon peel soaps around on the top. Summer took the shots quite close up, but making sure you could still see the cool old-fashioned writing on the side of the crate.

We put a heap of bath bombs in the old scales – soft pink rose and geranium ones with little rose buds in on one side, and powder blue ones full of lavender buds on the other. We put some of the Avocado Body Butter in a scooped-out avocado skin, sitting on a pile of whole ones, and we lined bottles of pink, yellow and purple bubble bath up in the window, so that the light came through them and really made the colours sing.

Then Summer decided that *I* should be in the Peppermint Kiss Lip Balm shots (I know, she must be blind! I'd have brought Saff down if I'd thought there'd be modelling involved!). Anyway, she got me to put some on, then smile whilst holding up a wooden box of bunches of mint with the little pots scattered amongst them. I just hoped I wouldn't look *too* awful in the finished shots – luckily my make-up had survived school okay so perhaps it would be alright. Ish.

Afterwards we went back to Summer's to have a look through the pictures properly on her computer. She lives out in the country, so her dad John picked us up in his ancient Land Rover (which, BTW, ran on old chip fat like on the wall display at school). John told me his job is advising businesses on going greener and using renewable energy, so he was one of the first round here to convert to biodiesel, the posh name for the old chip fat.

A couple of miles out of town, we turned off the main road and went bumping down a long dusty lane. We parked up outside a rambling cottage with sort of paddocky field things all around it. They had a few pigs and goats in, and a couple of donkeys. I felt a bit nervous. Summer's home seemed a world away from my place back in Ealing. I hoped I wouldn't make some massive un-environmental faux pas and offend her whole family.

I got out, tripped over some chickens which were just wandering about, and followed Summer through a cottage garden bursting with flowers and buzzing with bees. Then we walked up the path to the back door, through a massive veggie patch and a load of fruit canes under netting.

As we walked into the big farmhouse kitchen my brain struggled to take everything in. There was stuff everywhere – open shelves stacked with jars of grains, nuts, seeds and dried fruit, about ten different recycling bins, herbs hanging from the ceiling, postcards and cuttings all over the fridge, a clutter of plates and cups on the table, a dresser crammed with, well, just *stuff*, the smell of casserole or something coming from a pot on the big red Aga, two massive piles of laundry on the floor by the machine and two huge hairy dogs in their baskets.

And people, of course. The whole family was in there, chatting in a noisy, happy bustle that gave me a sharp pang in my stomach. *We used to be like that*, I thought, and then pushed the image of us all round our own table in Ealing out of my mind.

Summer introduced me to her mum Annie, and Jed and Jim her big, burly older brothers. I found out that Jed was in sixth form and Jim (who was sitting on a large dog-eared sofa, strumming a guitar) was doing a Countryside Management apprenticeship. Annie does crystal healing and chakra rebalancing, or crystal rebalancing and chakra healing, I can't remember which way round it was. Anyway, she gave me a big hug hello and said Summer had told her all about our business, and that I was welcome to anything from the garden that might be useful.

That was so nice of her and I said thanks loads, of course, and promised her free treatments in return, and we did the whole "Oh, that's not necessary", "Oh, but I insist" politeness thing (though I secretly planned to book her in and march her down there myself once we were open!). Then she stood back, peered at me and said, "Hmm, you're an Aquarius, yes?"

I nodded. "Wow, how did you know?" I asked.

"You'd have to have both creativity and determination to start your own business," she told me, "and Aquarians have those in abundance. They also hold strong during stormy times and they're protective of those they love."

I smiled back. I didn't know about *holding strong* during stormy times, but I seemed to be surviving them, at least. And the bit about being protective sounded about right. If that Richanne girl upset Grace again, she'd be sorry.

Annie filled the kettle and asked me what kind of tea I'd like.

"Erm, normal kind?" I replied, a bit confused.

"Oh, of course," she said, then started digging round in a cupboard packed with exotic-looking tea boxes and packets of dried herbs. "I'm sure we've got some somewhere," she muttered, "from when the builders were here."

"Don't worry, I'll have what you're having," I said quickly.

She made jasmine tea and we had it in mismatched vintage china cups with no saucers. It was such a delicate colour, and it smelled divine.

"We should offer some different teas at Rainbow Beauty," I said, thinking aloud. "Can you suggest some nice ones?"

Annie smiled. "I can do better than that." She started piling me up with boxes and herb sachets from the cupboard. "Take some of these home to try and then you can choose." It was so nice of her and I said thank you loads of times again.

"You know, what I could really do with is a good, natural gardeners' soap and a hand balm for chapped skin," she said then. "I bet a lot of other people round here would buy that too."

I smiled. "Thanks for the tip. I'll try and come up with something. I love a challenge."

Then Summer and I took our drinks up to her room. That was totally amazing too, with painted murals of Indian goddesses on the walls, bongos, an accordion, a pile of fabric floor cushions she'd made, and a colourful patterned rug over polished floorboards.

As we looked at the photos from the shoot (I had to admit I looked okay in the lip balm shots – phew!), we chatted about school and stuff. Then, "Were you seeing anyone back where you used to live?" Summer asked, as we sorted through the bubble bath images and shortlisted the best ones.

The way she said it – *where you used to live* – gave me a start. Even though I knew we weren't going home to our old life, that it was in the past now, part of me seemed to keep forgetting, and it gave me a jolt whenever I remembered.

I shook my head. "Nah. Me and my friends hung out with a few of the lads from the boys' school, but I wasn't *with* any of them."

"You must miss your old mates," she said then.

I shrugged. "I guess. But there's been so much going on, I've hardly had time to think about Em and

Zo." Of course, as soon as I said that, I suddenly missed them a *lot*. "I've sent them postcards, but they don't know I'm not coming back. It's been hard to keep in touch without a phone."

"Oh!" Summer gasped. "I can't believe I didn't think of that. Here." She rummaged in her pocket and handed me her mobile. "Call them now. Or you can message them on this in a minute." She gestured at the laptop.

Instead of jumping at the chance, I found myself saying thanks, but no thanks. I wouldn't have known where to begin, telling them what had happened. It would have been so awkward, with them not knowing what to say. And anyway, I didn't want to hear about everything I was missing. I remembered that there'd been a shopping trip to Kensington High Street planned for the Saturday just gone, and then afterwards we were all meeting Em's mum in town for a meal and going to see *Stomp* at the theatre. I realized I'd never be able to do stuff like that now, because it all cost money – not just for buying clothes and make-up and the theatre tickets, but for the trains and cabs, and lunch in Balans. I'd never even thought of all those little things before, but it added up to a lot.

"So, seems like things are hotting up with Marco," she said.

I couldn't help blushing. We hadn't really talked about the me-and-him thing since she'd told me about all those other girls. I knew she'd been hoping I'd cool things off with him after that, but she'd obviously noticed that I hadn't. "Actually I meant to ask you…" I began, trying to sound casual. "I've been thinking about what to wear to the gig – I want him to think I look good, but I don't want to seem like I'm trying too hard."

Summer sighed. "Oh, come on, Abs, he's so into you, he wouldn't care if you wore a bin bag."

I had to stop myself whooping with joy at that. "So you think he does like me then?" I asked, beaming. "I mean, I thought so, I *hoped* so, but I couldn't be sure, you know, cos he's such a flirt with everyone. But you know him really well, so if you think…"

Summer raised her eyebrows. "Well, don't expect it to come to anything, that's my advice," she said sternly. "Remember what I said about him and those other girls. He's into you now, that's obvious. But next week? Who knows."

She must have seen my face crumple, because she quickly added, "I'm only saying this because I care about you. You do know that, don't you, Abs? And it's nothing against Marco as a mate."

I felt like a massive idiot then. I'd been desperate to have a big giggly girly chat with her about him, but instead she was acting like a grumpy old granny. "It's no big deal," I stuttered.

All I wanted to do after that was change the subject, so I asked her about the uniform stuff she'd said I could have. She got it all out for me, and of course, being Summer's stuff, it looked as cool as uniform possibly can, and her washing powder smelled gorgeous too, of happiness and sunshine (I mean, lemon and bergamot!). I managed to get enough uniform bits to give Grace a set as well, even though I wasn't sure she'd be that grateful.

Then I asked Summer what *she* was wearing for the gig. She showed me and it was much more casual than I'd been expecting, just jeans and a T-shirt. "Thank goodness I saw your outfit," I told her. "I mean, I would have been stood there done up in a micro-mini and high heels, like we used to wear to the under-eighteens' night at Liquid."

Summer looked impressed. "Wow, did you really go clubbing in London? Cool! You must miss that!"

"Yeah," I mumbled. "I guess so."

She gave me a sad smile. "And, well, you must miss *everything*... How do you feel about what happened with your dad now?" she asked.

170

"Oh, I'm fine, I mean, I don't want to talk about it," I said automatically, but then I realized that I did. After all, I hadn't felt like I could say anything to Mum, Saff or Grace. It would be so good to let my feelings out. "Well, I feel like…" I paused, trying to put my finger on it – that scattered, floating, sick feeling I had in my head and stomach all the time. "I guess I felt completely safe and comfortable in our life and I thought it would always be there, and then everything changed, and it all suddenly ended, and it felt like…an earthquake, and…"

I paused. Summer was looking really anxious. I hadn't meant for that to happen. "It's completely different from your family," I said quickly. I realized then what a bad idea it had been to try and open up to her. She wouldn't understand at all – I mean, how could she? Suddenly, being in Summer's safe, solid, happy home made me feel even more lost and floaty than ever, and I just wanted to get back to the flat. "Oh, is that the time?" I asked, peering at her mobile. "I'd better head off. Mum's expecting me for dinner."

Jim offered to drive me back and Summer said she'd come with us, but I told them I fancied the walk. I didn't really want her seeing the flat yet, especially not now I'd seen how amazing her place was.

As we hugged goodbye, she said, "Make sure you stay right up on the grass verge on the bits where there's no pavement, and walk on the side with traffic coming towards you, apart from on blind corners, in which case cross over and—"

"Summer!" I cried, "I think I can walk two miles without getting myself run over!"

She grinned. "Well, you're such a city girl, I wasn't sure!"

As I headed off, I wondered if she was right. Was I still a city girl? I felt different somehow, since we'd been down here. I was still me, but not quite the same... Oh, it was too confusing to even think about, so as I strode along, I started coming up with ideas for how to display our products at Rainbow Beauty instead.

Chapter
Nine

On Tuesday morning, we were putting our leaflets together in Media class. When it came out that Ben had helped me in the greengrocer's at the weekend Marco got quite moody. "You should have told me, I would have helped too," he grumbled.

"Well, it wasn't planned—" I began.

"You had Saturday Music Club," Ben cut in, "and besides, Abbie needed someone strong."

Marco glared at him. "Huh! I'm stronger than you. Right, arm wrestle!"

"You sure?" said Ben. "We can't have you damaging your precious guitar-playing fingers before the gig, can we?"

"Dream on!" Marco growled. "It's you who'll be on your knees, begging for mercy!"

Luckily Mr. Mac came over then to see how we were doing, so they had to get on with their conservation group leaflet and stop acting like five year olds.

I ran into Grace in the corridor between lessons, and I almost didn't clock it was her at first because I'd forgotten she was wearing Summer's stuff (she'd surprised me by being okay about taking it). I told her she looked really nice, which she did – I mean, it would have helped if she'd taken down that harsh ponytail or put a bit of mascara on, but at least she was no longer rocking the pea-green posh girl look. I tried to get her to come and hang out with us at break, but she wouldn't. She didn't seem as unhappy as usual, though. She told me she'd mentioned the extension work to her Maths teacher, like we'd talked about, and that actually he'd been quite into the idea and said he'd see what he could do.

Mum seemed to be having a good day too – when I popped round to Liam's after school to get some money from her for milk and bread, I found them cosied up on the sofa in front of *The Wizard of Oz*. "Excuse me, I thought you were supposed to be working," I said sternly, but they hardly even looked up. They were just staring at the TV, mesmerized by Judy Garland singing "Over The Rainbow".

"Oh, she's so beautiful!" gasped Mum.

"I *so* love her!" cried Liam.

"Right, see you later then, I'm going now," I said, and when they didn't react, I added, "I'm off to nick a car and go joyriding up Fore Street."

Mum just murmured, "That's nice, love," which totally proved they weren't listening. I didn't mind, though. It was just so nice that she'd made a friend here. Things seemed to be working out okay for us – I just hoped Saff would get a place at college too, and then we'd all be happy. Well, getting back towards it at least. I wondered whether, somewhere out there, Dad was getting back towards happiness too. A mean little part of me hoped not, and another part missed him so much it made my stomach ache.

On Wednesday morning it was Saff's interview. She was really nervous about it – she had all of her clothes spread out on the bed, and for once Grace didn't complain about her side of the room being taken over. Saff tried on about twenty different combinations before finally settling on the first thing she'd picked out: a red vintage-y dress with some of

Mum's heels. We all wished her luck (except Grace who said "Break a leg" and nearly started another argument, until Mum explained that it actually meant "Good luck").

As Mum and I hugged Saff goodbye (Grace isn't big on hugging), Mum said, "I'll be sending you lots of positive energy this morning."

"OMG, you're going a bit Devon already, aren't you?" Saff giggled.

"You'll knock 'em dead," I told her, giving her an extra hug.

"Yeah, but try not to actually *kill* anyone, won't you?" added Grace, with a wicked grin.

Grace and I walked in to school together. When I got to our form room, my mates were already there, sitting on the desks, and when we all said hi Marco just grinned and handed me a massive clinking bag.

It turned out he'd been to the big spa hotel at the edge of town, and a couple of the smaller central ones, and asked if he could have all their used little glass jam and marmalade pots for my free samples, so I could save on buying them from the specialist supplier.

"Oh wow, this is brilliant!" I cried.

"Calm down, it's no big deal," he mumbled, blushing.

"Yes, it is," I said. "You're a star, thank you."

"He's even washed them all out and soaked the labels off," said Summer, "so we can make sheets of Rainbow Beauty ones on the colour copier in the library, then cut them out and stick them on."

"Cool, Grace has given me the list of official ingredient names we have to use, so we can start this lunchtime," I told her.

"Aw, I bet you got a *Blue Peter* badge when you were little, didn't you mate?" Ben teased.

"I got two, mate," said Marco. He looked so awkward and cute, I could have hugged him. In fact, I was just about to, but Mrs. Lurman walked in.

Later on, in the corridor just after French, something even more amazing than Marco collecting all the jars for me happened. The two of us were first out of the lesson, and we were walking along on our own and, for the record, his *exact* words were: "Abs, do you feel like coming to our gig tomorrow night?"

Well, I didn't say anything back at first, because I was too busy stopping myself from screaming my head off and dancing around like a total crazy person, going "Yes, yessity, yes, yes!" Then when I did speak, my mouth was so completely dry that my voice came out in a weird croaky whisper. And I knew I was going to sound like a sad case, but I had to make absolutely sure he did mean what I *thought* he meant. "Erm, Summer invited me already, remember?" I said.

"Oh, that's cool," he mumbled, shoving his hands into the pockets of the black skinny jeans that passed for school trousers. "If you'd rather go with her then…"

"No, I didn't mean that, I'm just saying, I was already planning on coming, so…"

"I know you were. I meant, come *with* me." He looked really uncomfortable that he was having to spell it out. Poor boy, and I was about to make it even worse for him. "What, like, as in a *date*?" I asked.

OMG, how uncool, but I just had to double-triple-check.

He shrugged. "Yeah. Kind of thing."

I nearly couldn't control the "Yes, yessity, yes, yes!" dance then, and I ended up bobbing about a little bit, so I had to act out this whole thing of frowning at my foot and shaking it, pretending there was something in my shoe. "Okay, cool, then…erm, I mean, yes, I accept your invitation to go on a date, kind of thing." Urgh! Geek alert! Still, at least there was no possible confusion. He had asked me and I had said yes.

While I was still behaving like a total weird girl, doing the foot-shaking thing, he said "See ya" and went off down the corridor, so then I *did* get to do my air-punching happy dance. I stopped when Summer appeared round the corner, but I couldn't help grinning like a maniac.

"Erm, what's going on?" she asked, peering at me.

"Oh, nothing much, us two are going to the gig together, that's all." I said it as casually as I could, gesturing towards Marco's back as he loped down the corridor.

"What, *together* together?"

"Yeah. As in a date. Kind of thing."

Summer gasped and I felt really anxious. "Erm, why the shock-horror?" I demanded.

"He asked you out!" she cried. "That must have made him squirm! Normally he makes the girls do all the running. Maybe things *are* different with you, Abs."

I raised my eyebrows and she held her hands up. "Okay, okay! I'm officially giving him the benefit of the doubt."

I had to force my mouth not to go into a ginormous grin when I heard that. Summer saying that it looked like Marco had changed was *massive*, but I tried to act like the whole thing was no big deal. "I'm still not going to take it too seriously, though," I said. Ahem. LIE. "It's not like I'm that into him or anything." Ahem. MASSIVO LIE. "But a date kind of thing might be fun after all the serious stuff going on with my family." Okay, so that was true at least.

Summer didn't have to know that there was something really special between me and Marco. I'd felt such a strong connection, right from the first moment I met him, and I'm sure he had too. And I'd told myself that the reason he was a flirt and had lots of girls hanging round him was because he hadn't met the right one yet (i.e. *moi!*). Well, Summer had said it herself – I was different. Now I'd made *him* different.

That night me, Mum, Saff and Grace were all cleaning out the shop. Saff's interview had gone well (and so had her friend Emily's) but she'd banned us from talking about it in case we jinxed it. She said she just wanted to put it out of her mind until she heard back.

I wasn't going to tell them about my D.A.T.E. because I knew they'd only tease me and go on and on about it, but as I tackled the disgusting loo (with two pairs of rubber gloves on and a scarf around my face), I noticed Saff peering suspiciously at me. "You

180

look very happy for a girl who's scrubbing out The Most Revolting Toilet In The World," she said. "Come on, spill los beanios."

And then Mum joined in, trying to guess what my secret was, and in the end I gave them all a cheeky grin and put on a bossy voice and said, "I'll tell you when all that broken furniture's piled up in the skip outside and not before."

"Oh, you're cruel, Abbie Green," said Mum, poking me in the ribs. "You know we'll do anything for a bit of juicy gossip."

Half an hour later the skip was full and they were back on my case. "You do realize I've chipped a nail," moaned Saff, "so this had better be worth it!"

So I told them about how Marco had asked me to the gig AS A DATE and they all got totally over-the-top excited.

"Is he fit?" (Saff, of course.)

"*Oh* yes."

"Is he clever?" (You can guess who said that.)

"Mmm-hmm."

"Is he your age?" That was Mum.

I nodded. "Yeah. He's in my form. I got lost on my way to class and he kind of rescued me from the storm." My stomach flipped over, remembering Marco's blazer around me, the first time I saw his smile, us holding hands as we ran through the rain. "He's the first person I met on my first day," I told them.

"Oh, *choosy*!" sneered Grace.

I stuck my tongue out, and Saff said, "Ignore her, I bet it was fate. You *have* to get together now, cos you've got such an amazing getting-together story! What are you going to wear to the gig? How are you doing your make-up and hair?"

Those were good questions. What *do* you wear to be the girlfriend of a rock god? Oh, hang on, *girlfriend*? Maybe I was jumping the gun a bit... But then, perhaps I *would* be his girlfriend after the D.A.T.E. "Well, I'm not sure—" I began.

"What?" Saff screeched. "How can you not be *prepared*? It's tomorrow night!"

"Well, I did pack my black dress and I thought maybe if I could borrow your silver boots..." I said. "But then Summer's just wearing jeans and a T-shirt so maybe I should go more casual..."

"Good for her," Grace said. "She doesn't feel she has to dress for male approval, and neither should you."

I didn't point out to her that Summer's so naturally beautiful she could turn up in my hideous too-short puppy PJs and still look like she'd stepped off the cover of *Zest* mag. I couldn't have got a word in anyway, even if I'd wanted to, because Saff was gabbling away, telling Grace not to be so stuffy and adding, "Anyway, Summer's not going to be there on a date with the future love of her life. Abbie *is*!"

I thought my inner glow was turned up to maximum already, but when Saff said that I felt it notch up even more. If we could have bottled that feeling and sold it at Rainbow Beauty we'd have been millionaires.

"The black dress really suits you, but you're right, it might be a bit done-up for down here," said Saff thoughtfully. "Maybe if you wore some skinny jeans under it, and lots of strings of pearls… When we get back upstairs, let's have a look through my stuff and see what we can put together."

"Oh, thanks, sis, that would be amazing!" I cried. I gave her a big hug then, and she went hysterical because I was still wearing the loo-contaminated rubber gloves.

The next evening, I was so excited about the D.A.T.E. I actually had to stop myself skipping down the pavement when Summer's car pulled up. Saff and I had put a fantastic outfit together the night before (the skinny jeans and dress had worked out well, with Saff's red shoes with roses on) and I hoped I looked nice. Summer said I did anyway, when I got in the back seat, and Ben didn't throw up or anything.

They'd been right about Dartington, it was totally gorgeous. It was a grand old hall on the outside but this cool venue on the inside.

"There's a cinema here too, and they have a theatre," Ben told me as we walked up to the entrance.

"We'll have to go and see something soon," said Summer.

We all went in and got drinks from the trestle table they'd set up at the back and after a while Marco came over. I was a bit surprised that he just said hey to all of us and didn't say a special hello to me or give me a hug. And he didn't even mention my outfit. But then, he did look a bit stressed, and he soon rushed off to sort some band stuff out, so I decided we'd probably just hang out properly (you know, on our D.A.T.E.) after their set.

We said hi to loads of other people from our class and Summer introduced me to some girls who were in our year that she used to do netball club with. By the time things got started it felt like most of the upper school was there, plus Marco's brigade of Year Eight female fans, of course. *Oh, well,* I thought, *they can enjoy it for one last night until me and him are together for good.*

Headrush were on first and they were really good – after all Ben and Summer's teasing, I'd kind of expected them not to be. It was brilliant, dancing along in the crowd, and I loved watching Marco play (I'd been right – total licence to stare!). He was so into it and just seemed completely lost in what he was doing, like I get when I'm inventing beauty recipes (except that I don't mosh about and end up dripping with sweat!).

When he came straight over to us after their set (and the two extra songs the crowd made them do) he winked at me and I thought everything was going to be fine after all. But no – he just hung around long enough for me to tell him how good it was, and then he was off, flirting with the Year Eights. Then the whole band came over to him and they were all chatting and joking about with the girls and he stayed put even when the next band came on, like he wasn't *with* me at all. I tried to pretend that I was too busy listening to the music to care *what* he was doing, but it obviously didn't work because Summer nudged me and said, "Why don't you go and hang out with them?"

"But I don't know them," I said lamely.

"You've talked to Declan in the lunch hall, and we

always say hi to Tay and Chaz when we see them round school," she countered.

So I took a deep breath, and pulled on a smile, and went over. I was standing right beside Marco but apart from a quick glance, he acted like I wasn't there! I said hi to Declan and introduced myself properly to Tay and Chaz. We chatted a bit and I thought Marco would join in and mention that I was there with him, but he didn't, so they probably thought I was just some random fan.

I wanted to start up a proper conversation with them but I was SO annoyed with Marco by then that my brain went completely blank, and in the end I was just standing there in silence like a total idiot. My mind went into overdrive then, thinking, *What's up with him? Aren't I cool enough for him? If he changed his mind, why didn't he have the guts to say so at school? I got all excited, told my family, dressed up...*

Honestly, I felt so stupid, especially because I knew my friends were watching me (oh, as well as – did I mention? – *half the school*). What would Summer say? I couldn't stand the thought of her and Ben feeling sorry for me.

Eventually though, the embarrassment of standing there like a lemon got so bad that I had to go back over to Summer and Ben. Yes, they *did* look gutted for me — how cringe-making! "I think I'm going to head off," I said, as casually as I could.

I started to walk away, but, "Hang on," said Summer, "how will you get home?"

I shrugged. "I'll be fine. It's light till ten, and it's only a couple of miles along the river path." Then I added, "So you don't have to worry about me getting run over," trying to sound all jokey, like I was fine.

"Don't be silly, you're not walking back on your own," said Ben, going all macho on me. "I'll come with you."

"We'll all go," said Summer. "I'll ring my dad to pick us up now."

"No, you two are having a good time," I said. "I'll be fine." But they were both just giving me stern looks and I realized they weren't going to back down. I was quite relieved, actually — I didn't really fancy walking all that way on my own, in a place I didn't know, without a phone or Mum knowing where I was. "Okay, look, I'll stay," I said, "but I'm going to have a walk around outside, get some air."

Ben and Summer looked at each other. "Fine, then we'll come with you," Ben said. "I'll show you the cool Zen Garden."

"Good idea. I bet you could do with a little Zen right now," said Summer, throwing a poisonous look at Marco, which he didn't even notice because he was too wrapped up in his fan club. Argh! I wanted to just melt into a puddle on the floor and never be seen or heard of again. "I'm so sorry, hon," Summer said then. "I really did hope he'd be different with you. But he's such an immature idiot, he just had to mess you around and ruin things." Thank goodness she seemed to notice that I was *dying of embarrassment* then and stopped going on about it. "You two go," she said. "I really need the loo. I'll catch you up in a sec."

As soon as Ben and I were outside, I let all my frustration out. The Zen Garden was gorgeous, but it didn't stand a chance of making me feel chilled, not with the mood I was in.

"Seriously, tell me the truth," I ranted at poor Ben as we walked along amongst the beautiful flowers, next to the tranquil pond. "Am I so hideous that you'd ask me on a date and then change your mind when I arrive?"

"Oh, there are some lovely koi carp in here," he said.

"Ben! Focus!" I snapped. "Am I hideous? I mean, *look* at me!"

Reluctantly, he glanced up from the pond. "It's nothing to do with how you look—" he began, but, seeing my face cloud over, he added quickly, "Not that you don't look, you know...*well fit.*" He said that in a laddish way, trying to make me laugh, but I just glared at him, so he shrugged and went back to Fish Watch.

"So, why's he being like this then?" I demanded. "Does he think I'm not cool enough for him? He obviously doesn't like me if he's acting this way, so why did he even ask me out?"

"I don't know," Ben muttered. "Because he's an idiot, probably. Abs, look at the relaxing fish."

"What, you think he was an idiot to ask me out in the first place?"

Ben looked alarmed. "No, I didn't say that! I mean, he's an idiot to act like this. Oh look, a ghost carp. Quite a big one too."

"So, do you think he never really liked me anyway?"

"*What?*" cried Ben, finally giving up on his fish therapy. "What are you *on* about? Bloody hell, girls can be proper mental sometimes. *Course* he likes you, Abs. He never asks anyone out – he lets the girls do the chasing – but he asked *you*. So he must like you, right?"

"Huh! That's what Summer said! Well, he's got a funny way of showing it!" I snarled. "Anyway, I don't care what he thinks any more because that's the end of it. *Finito*. I felt like such an idiot in there, with him ignoring me and flirting with all those girls. I can't be bothered with his stupid games. I've got far too much to deal with in my life already. I need to be with someone straightforward who's not going to mess me around... Actually I'll probably just go off boys altogether and become a nun. I've got three pairs of those disgusting tights left, shame to waste them."

Ben smirked. "Do you reckon nuns are allowed to wear make-up, though?" he asked. "You don't want to be known as the headless nun of Totnes."

I slapped him.

"Ow!" he cried. "Hey! You're *always* saying that!"

"Yeah, well, it's MY headlessness!" I fired back. "Doesn't mean *you* can comment on it, *bandy legs*!" I did an impression of him walking, swaying from side to side. Outraged, he nudged me into a bush, and I slapped him one again.

Thank goodness for good mates.

"Look, sorry for taking it out on you," I said then. "I'm just so annoyed with myself. Summer did warn me about Marco — I should have listened."

Ben shrugged. "Yeah, well, live and learn. Don't give up on blokes, though, will you? We're not all the same."

"Okay, if you say so."

"I do."

Just then I spotted Summer waving to us from the doorway. "Guys, the headliner's coming on!" she called.

"Thanks for coming outside with me, and cheering me up," I said as Ben and I headed back into the hall. "Don't tell Marco I was annoyed though, will you? Just say I had a bad stomach—" I paused, realizing that whatever I thought of Marco, I didn't want him picturing me sat on the loo with exploding diarrhoea. "No, hang on, a headache, say a headache," I said. "I don't want him thinking this bothered me. I feel enough of an idiot already."

When we got back in, Marco did come and hang out with us, but I pretty much ignored him by pretending I was too into the music to notice him trying to catch my eye.

When the headline act finished their set, us four headed out on the stream of people and Summer spotted her dad's Land Rover. "Do you want a lift back?" she asked Marco, but he said he had to stay and help load the drum kit and stuff into Declan's dad's van. So us three said "See ya", and he was kind of hovering around, but I didn't hug him or anything, I just got into the Land Rover and didn't look back.

Yes, Ben had cheered me up a bit, but it didn't last long. Because when I got in, I stupidly ended up telling Mum, Saff and Grace what had happened.

Grace muttered gravely about how I shouldn't have got distracted from Rainbow Beauty and my schoolwork by a boy in the first place (yeah, thanks, really helpful, sis!). Even worse, Saff got all worked up on my behalf and wanted to go and have it out with Marco. I don't know what she was planning to do as we didn't own anything weapon-like. Maybe pelt him with wellies? And Mum decided that just because Marco and Dad have acted like idiots, All Men Are The Same.

I wanted to say "Ben's not" but I knew they'd take that to mean I fancied him, and ignore me saying we're just mates, so I kept my mouth shut. Then I went to take my make-up off, wondering how we'd all be able to hang out tomorrow at school as normal when I didn't feel like speaking to Marco ever again.

I couldn't believe how stupid I'd been, and that I'd ignored Summer's warnings. I should have been hearing warning bells – big, loud, clanging ones with a computerized voice like they have on delivery vans – saying, "Abbie Green! Step Away From The Egotistical Ratbag!"

What had I been thinking? Well, I hadn't been thinking at all, obviously. Instead I'd switched off my brain and been drawn in by a floppy black fringe, a slow, knowing smile, and the gorgeous warm, spicy smells of cinnamon and musk. Even now, after the Total Humiliation of being MDP (as me, Em and Zo used to call it – i.e. Massively Dissed in Public), I found myself staring in the mirror, thinking about being wrapped in his blazer that first day, our hands touching, that zap of electricity…

Argh! What was wrong with me?! Of *course* he was charming. That was the whole point. I rubbed hard at my layers of black-and-silver eye make-up with a cleansing wipe and disappeared once again into headlessness. Well, his charm might work on the rest of the girls at school – but not me.

Not any more.

I promised myself that the next day I'd be friendly and polite, of course – I didn't want to make things awkward for Summer and Ben. But apart from that, there would be nothing between us. *Nada*. No spark, no fizz, no secret smiles. There was no point being moody or sulky, I'd just make it clear in a massively mature way that I was SO over it with him. I'd be immune to his beautiful playful eyes and never again casually touch his hand or link arms with him. Ha! That'd teach him to mess with Abbie Green. I'd go in there with the strident feminist principles of Grace (and of course, the drop-dead gorgeous hair and make-up of Saff – no harm in showing him what he was missing!) and be such an ice queen he'd think the school boiler was broken.

Erm…yeah, right.

When I got in to school on Friday morning, I *was* all set up for my ice maiden routine, but I was really thrown because, weirdly, Marco seemed to be in a mood with *me*. I decided he was still playing his stupid games and I'd just have to rise even higher above it all.

Which was all good and fine – until Science.

OMG, it was SO cringe-making that I just wanted to get the sulphuric acid out and dissolve myself into a puddle on the floor. Us four were supposed to be working as a group, but Marco was acting like he was in charge and getting me to pass him stuff, as if I was some kind of lab assistant. That really annoyed me, and I guess I was passing the things quite *hard*, because the glass rod snapped in his hand.

"Ow!" he cried, nursing his palm.

"Oh, don't be such a baby," I hissed.

"You did that on purpose," he accused.

"Course I didn't," I spat. "Not everything's about *you*, you know."

We glared at each other as he rubbed his hand.

"Well, this isn't awkward at all, is it?" said Ben cheerily.

Then Marco noticed Summer glaring at him and turned on her. "Oi, don't give me the evils! What have *I* done?"

"As if you didn't know!" she muttered. She put her arm round me but I wriggled away and marched over to the shelves for a new glass rod.

Summer followed. "That boy – what a nightmare!" she grumbled. "It's time he learned he can't treat people like—"

"Look, thanks for standing up for me and everything," I cut in, "but I'm fine, really. I don't want to go into it with him, and I definitely don't want *you* to go into it with him, in the middle of a *lesson*. I love hanging out with you guys. Let's not ruin the group over nothing."

She grimaced. "Okay, fair enough."

"I know you warned me," I said, "and I should have listened. Luckily I wasn't that into him." *Whoopsie, LIE again.* "Or I might be gutted right now. But it was no big deal, okay?" *Oh dear, another one.* "Let's just move on."

"Okay," said Summer, "if you're really sure. Although, he SO deserves a—"

"I'm sure," I said firmly. "It was just a stupid mistake. That's the end of it. Definitely."

Chapter Ten

The weekend was our big chance to get loads done on Rainbow Beauty. Mum and Saff had been down there every day, cleaning and sorting out, so by Saturday morning the kitchen area was spotless (the tiles had turned out to be a completely different colour once they were cleaned – a nicer one, luckily), the windows were sparkling and all the safety signs, first-aid stuff and fire extinguishers were stacked up ready to be put in their places.

We'd already put most of the rubbish, like the yucky old blinds, paper files and gross bin (and sexist calendar), into the skip Liam had ordered. Mum and Saff had made a start on preparing the walls for decorating, and sanded back the skirting boards, and we were planning to get the place completely painted over the weekend. The velvet sofas Mum had ordered had arrived, and were safely under their plastic wrapping and two huge dust sheets.

I'd seen a chiller counter advertised in the local paper and phoned up about that too. I'd had the idea of putting the fresh face masks and smoothie ingredients in it, displayed really nicely, maybe on ice or with flowers round, to make a cool feature in the reception area. It was only thirty quid, and I'd been so excited I'd found myself just calling up and asking about the size, and then saying I'd have it.

I knew Ben and Summer were coming to help out (although Summer couldn't stay long because she was going camping with her family). Marco had said he'd come too, but that was before the gig. As things were so awkward between us I'd just assumed he wouldn't show his face (I hadn't stabbed him with any more glass rods but we still weren't properly speaking). So I had a big shock when he came striding in with Ben. As usual, my stomach flipped over just from looking at Marco, annoyingly, and I found myself wishing I wasn't in my decorating gear of a pea-green old school shirt and my worst jeans. Only to show him what he was missing, of course, not to impress him or anything.

I introduced Marco to everyone and Ben to Mum, and soon the boys were busy arguing over who was going to lift this really heavy desk that we hadn't managed to get into the skip. They were both insisting they could do it without the other's help and even when they eventually decided to work together, they still couldn't shift it. That was when Summer strolled in, with her big brothers in tow. Once again, I felt like shutting Saff's mouth for her, as it was hanging open at the sight of Jed and Jim.

"Just in time," she said, giving them her sultriest smile, "some real men."

"Oh, thanks very much!" grumbled Marco.

"Fair point, though," said Summer. "I didn't think two puny boys would be much use in this situation, so I brought some muscle along."

By the time she and Marco had finished bickering about whether or not he was puny, Jed and Jim had the desk in the skip. Then Liam pulled up outside in his van and they went striding off to help him unload.

"I'll get out there and give them a hand," said Marco, making for the door. But Mum intercepted him. "I think they've got the heavy lifting covered," she said, giving him a wicked smile. "But if you could

198

get the cobwebs off the ceiling that would be wonderful," she added, handing him a feather duster. Ha ha! She obviously hadn't forgiven him for what happened at the gig.

While Marco was staring at the fluffy pink duster in horror, she handed Ben a Stanley knife. "And if you could get this old carpet ripped up, Ben, love, that would be brilliant."

"Yes, of course, Mrs. Green," said Ben, weighing the knife in his hand and looking smugly at Marco, who grumbled, "Hang on, why does he get a knife and I—"

But he got cut off by us girls all greeting Liam as he staggered in clutching a box with some pieces of glass sticking out of the top. "Morning all!" he cried, leaning it against the wall and going over to Marco and Ben. "Hi, I'm Liam," he said, grinning and holding out his hand.

When the introductions were over, he said, "That glass is going to be shelves for your product sales. And this is for the juice bar," he added, as Jed and Jim burst in with a long bit of countertop that looked like it weighed a ton and put it down before they dropped it.

"But we can't afford this!" Mum shrieked. "It's granite, it must have cost a fortune."

"It was gratis," said Liam, beaming. "I've just done a kitchen refurb and the clients let me have it."

"But how could anyone throw this out?" Mum gasped, stroking it lovingly. "There's not a scratch on it!"

Liam shrugged. "It just wasn't to their taste. They moved into this smartly-done place and they wanted the cottagey look."

"What a waste," said Mum, "although I have to admit I'd have done the same kind of thing a few months ago. Oh well, our gain. Thank you so, so much, Liam."

"You're welcome," Liam said proudly. "But that's not all, because I managed to blag the kitchen stools as well." He gestured towards the door where Jed and Jim were heading back in with four smart cream leather bar stools. Mum was totally wowed, and started going on about what good quality they were. "I got them in return for fitting their bathroom lights," Liam told her. "And two free massages for the lady of the house – I hope that's okay."

"Yes, of course!" Mum cried.

Liam beamed. "Good, because in the van I've got two chests of drawers that they were chucking out too. I thought they looked perfect for the treatment rooms and I promised her a luxury pedicure and a full body treatment for them."

Mum was hugging him by then, and just saying thank you over and over again. Me, Saff and Grace all said thank you loads too, and I had a go on one of the cool bar stools. Then Jed and Jim went back out with Liam for the chests of drawers, Ben made a start on ripping up the revolting hairy carpet and Mum, Saff and Grace got back to preparing the walls for painting. Once the van was unloaded, Jed, Jim and Summer had to head off. So, after we'd all said our goodbyes and Saff had finally put her tongue back in, I was left standing there with Marco, him still holding the offending feather duster and neither of us knowing what to say.

Luckily Liam was ready to go to the DIY store then and we'd planned that I'd go with him, because I was in charge of the colour scheme. As well as paint, we had loads of other stuff to get, like the laminate flooring, the underlay for it, and the light fittings and lamps for the treatment rooms. He was going to use his trade discount to get it all cheaper for us. "I could do with one of you lads to help load the van at the other end," he said, just as we were walking out of the door.

Ben leaped up but Marco threw down the feather

duster, muttered, "I'll go," and strode out of the door before anyone could argue. He sat in the back seat, so I got in the front next to Liam. I mean, it was nice that he'd turned up, but I wasn't planning to make a special effort to be friendly or anything.

It was so cool when we got to the DIY store because under the canopy bit by the entrance, there was this recycling promotion. You could bring in old paint you weren't going to use, or help yourself to whichever tins you wanted from the pile. I was so excited, realizing that if I looked through the huge stack really carefully, I might be able to get most of the paint for free. I had a good hunt for the perfect pink (I'd been planning to do the whole place in a gorgeous rich magenta) but I soon realized that most of the tins were at least half empty.

When I saw how nice the possible purples I'd rooted out and lined up looked together I had the idea to use more colours, maybe even all the colours of the rainbow, if the tones worked. So, as well as the purples, I picked out a couple of violets and a deep indigo, a scarlet, a big tin of burnt orange, a rich yolk yellow and a moss green. There was some lovely vintage grey for the woodwork and units too, so in the end we only had to pay for two massive tubs of trade white undercoat.

Things seemed to be going so well – the way it was all coming together made it feel like Rainbow Beauty was meant to be. When Marco came to get me to look at the different shades of laminate flooring (Liam wasn't sure which would go best with my new colour scheme), I couldn't help giving him a massive grin.

He peered at me suspiciously. "Erm, Abs, you do know this is *me* you're grinning at, don't you?" he asked.

"I know," I said, suddenly really wanting to put all the silly resentment behind us, rather than just *pretending* I had. "Look, let's just forget about what happened, yeah?" I said, as I followed him into the store. "I want to focus on Rainbow Beauty now."

"Sure," he said. "Yeah. Whatever. Cool."

I realized that that was as close to an apology from him as I was going to get, and decided it would have to do. I grinned and nudged him. "I reckon I'll just pick whichever flooring's the heaviest," I said. "It'll be funny watching you trying to get it in the van."

"You cheeky cow!" he cried, nudging me back.

It was really nice for us two to just be back to normal with no weird edginess between us. I did have to remind myself not to get *too* back to normal though, because for us normal meant me flirting with him and "accidentally" touching him, and staring at him when he wasn't looking. I had to find a new normal. A just-mates kind of normal.

On the way back we stopped off to collect the chiller counter. The fishmonger I'd bought it from hadn't mentioned that it weighed a ton, and it was hilarious watching Liam lift one end easily as Marco struggled with the other. I did try to help him but he wouldn't have any of it, so I relaxed on the pavement and made a few skinny indie boy jokes instead.

Fitting the counter into the back of the van meant piling the back seat up with some of our stuff, so we ended up all having to go in the front for the rest of the journey. The passenger bench seat was *designed* to fit two people, but it was still a bit of a squash, and every time Liam went round a corner, I ended up leaning into Marco and getting swirled up in his gorgeous smell, which made my heart pound fast and my stomach start flipping. *Don't get any ideas, Abbie Green*, I told myself sternly. *Think about how badly he showed you up at the gig. Friend, yes. Anything more, absolute no-no.*

Well, that seemed to work. I shuffled away from him and gripped the door handle instead of his arm when Liam took the corners too fast. Also, when

Katy Perry came on the radio singing "Hot N Cold", me and Liam joined in at the tops of our voices, and I didn't even care if Marco thought we were lame. When it got to the chorus, I just looked at him, raised my eyebrows and gave him a wicked grin, as if the song was talking about *him*. I just wanted him to realize that I knew exactly what he was like with girls, and that I wasn't bothered about him in that way any more.

Back at the shop, we cracked on and got loads done, and Marco and Ben didn't leave till half eight, after we'd had our takeaway pizzas (I made sure I said "See ya" to Marco in the same way as I did to Ben, so he didn't think he was getting any special treatment). I split a double pepperoni with Saff as usual and it was really nice, us all sitting on the floor admiring our work (Mum wouldn't let any of us near the purple velvet sofas!).

Mum and Saff had finished preparing the walls for paint and got two white undercoats on so that we could get the colours up first thing in the morning. Meanwhile, Grace had been upstairs filling out health and safety forms and packaging our samples up for the cosmetic chemist to test (she came back down for her fave ham and mushroom pizza though). When everyone had gone home or back upstairs, I sat in the middle of the shop floor with the different paint colours brushed onto bits of paper all around me, and worked out how best to do the colour scheme. Then I just sat there and gazed at everything we'd done so far, and I felt like pinching myself to make sure I wasn't dreaming.

On Sunday, it was just me, Mum, Saff, Grace and Liam at the shop, but still, it was amazing how much we got done. Liam laid the floor with Grace's help (she worked out all the cutting angles and marked the boards up for him so he could just crack on with the actual fitting). Luckily he'd thought to get the click-down not the glue-down kind, so we could walk on it straight away.

I'd decided not to go for a complete rainbow of colours in the end, because I was worried it would look like a children's nursery, but I planned to layer different violets, purples and indigos on the walls, doors, woodwork and shelves. I'd offset that with the rich yolk yellow on the reception desk, aged down with sandpaper and a thin layer of gold. And I'd put the mossy green on the wall behind the rich purple velvety sofas. I had the burnt orange left over, because it was just too much with all the other colours, but maybe we'd be able to use it for something later on. The painting took us the whole of Sunday, and we'd have to give it all another coat and do some touching up during the week, but it already looked amazing.

By the end of the weekend, the transformation was almost complete. Yes, Liam's electrician mate still needed to come in and wire up the lights, and the shelves had to be painted and fitted, and there were about a million other tiny jobs to finish off, but the reception sofas, treatment couches and chests of drawers were in place and Liam had almost finished fitting the juice bar. By eight o'clock on Sunday night we were all completely knackered. As we sat in the middle of the floor with cups of tea and fish and chips, I felt filled with this kind of sparkly glow.

Rainbow Beauty was real. With vision, creativity, a little help from our friends and a lot of hard work, we'd made it happen.

Now we just had to make it a success.

Chapter
Eleven

We were busy all week making products, putting
the finishing touches to the parlour, and delivering
the leaflets Summer and I had designed around the
neighbourhood. Saff did a two-day manicure summer
course at the college and came back with a diploma
so that she could help Mum with clients' nails when
we opened. By Wednesday night the phone line was
connected, we'd finished all the painting, the till was
set up and Liam's electrician had checked over the
wiring (luckily it wasn't as bad as we'd thought).
He'd also put the new lights and smoke alarms up
for us, in return for free treatments for his wife when
we opened. Once the washing machine had been

plumbed into the little kitchen (for free, thanks to Liam's mate Gordon the plumber, now the proud owner of a complete set of Rainbow Beauty products for his new girlfriend), Mum had washed all the new towels and arranged them in the chests of drawers.

The shelves were up but we still had to stock them with products. We'd passed our health and safety inspection with flying colours (phew!) – they just needed Mum to send them the electrical safety certificate and we were in business. We weren't setting all the stuff up in the fridge unit until Friday, but the smoothie bar was finished, with the juicer and blender gleaming on the granite counter. Summer's handwritten chalkboard sign telling customers all about the juices and smoothies hung on the wall above it.

Things were coming together for Grace and Saff too. Grace told me that when Mr. Hayes had announced to the entire class that he was setting up a lunchtime Extended Maths group because "Grace Green has asked for extra work", she'd wished the ground would open up and swallow her. But then two others, Aran and Maisy, had hung back after class and asked to join. Grace had been to lunch with them that day, and again the next, and she was beginning to believe they might want to be friends with her.

As for Saff, she'd had a call from Sally, the tutor she'd hit it off with at the college. Apparently she'd done really well on the practical tests as well as the interview bit and they were offering her a place. She was still panicking about her grades, but Sally had told her just to wait and see, and that if they weren't up to scratch they could still discuss options like Saff retaking her Maths and English GCSEs alongside her first year on the course. So she was much happier after that, knowing that there would still be options even if she hadn't done that well in her exams.

Every day I woke up and the first thought I had (apart from *Curse this spiny mattress!*) was: *Five days till the grand opening... Four days... Three days...* I hardly noticed that it was the last week of term, despite the special prize-giving assembly, mass shirt-signings and silly-string battles erupting everywhere. Preparing for the launch of Rainbow Beauty was taking up most of my time – Summer and I spent every break and lunch doing the labels and typing up the product information sheets for Grace's master file. Writing the labels was taking ages, as we had to look up all the official ingredient names, but luckily Mrs. Warner in the library had been brilliant, showing us how to scan our label designs into the computer and then print pages of them straight out onto sticky labels rather than using the photocopier.

After school each afternoon we were all busy sitting round the kitchen table working out the timings and pricing for the treatments, or making more products, or downstairs putting the finishing touches in place, like pictures and plants. So I didn't have much time to think about Marco. We still worked together in class sometimes, and Summer and I grabbed lunch with him and Ben before heading to the library, but that was it. Still, the just-being-friends thing seemed to be going okay.

At least, I thought so, until we were on our way to Geography on Wednesday after last break. We just happened to be walking together, and suddenly Marco said, "Do you fancy going to the cafe tomorrow night? Just for something to eat. No big deal."

Well, that caught me completely by surprise.

"What, on our own?" I asked.

"Well, I was thinking more *together*," he said.

"Oh, right!" I said. "Sorry, I meant, as in not with Summer and Ben."

"I know, I was joking," he said.

"Oh," I said. "What, about the Summer and Ben thing, or about us going in the first place?" I know! What an idiot! But I had to check.

"The Summer and Ben thing," he said. He laughed nervously. "Oh dear, this isn't going too well, is it?"

"It's fine," I mumbled. "It's just I..." I was about to say no, after what had happened at the gig and everything, but then I thought, *Why not? I mean, it's only the cafe. I probably won't even bother getting dressed up.*

"I just have to go back to the flat first, so I can't come straight out after school," I told him. "We've got stuff to do, for the opening."

He smiled at me. "So that's a yes then, is it?"

"Yeah, sure, whatever," I said, finally managing to dredge up a bit of cool from somewhere, even though it was way too late for that.

"Great. Well, I've got band practice till six, but I'm free then if that works for you."

"That's fine," I told him, just as we reached our lesson and I realized we'd been dawdling so much that everyone else was already sitting down with their books out.

As I hurried to my seat, I told myself firmly that I was only giving Marco one final chance – if he blew it again, that was it. I knew that Summer would think I was a pushover, so I decided not to mention it to her. I was planning to see how it went first. If he told her, fair enough (although I didn't think he would

212

somehow!). It'd be such a different situation from the gig, with just me and him, and we'd get a chance to properly talk to each other on our own. It wasn't even like an actual *date* anyway – just a hanging-out kind of thing.

Of course, when I got back to the flat and told my family, they didn't take it as just a hanging-out kind of thing – they took it as a MASSIVE BIG DEAL kind of thing. I had to tell them that what had happened at the gig was just a complete misunderstanding (okay, not exactly true, but easier than persuading them to give Marco another chance, especially Saff). Once I'd done that, they were totally on board (well, mostly).

In all the excitement, it was somehow decided that as we needed to do a test run of Rainbow Beauty, and that as I had a (just hanging-out kind of) date to get ready for, *I'd* be the pretend customer.

So when Grace and I got in from school on Thursday (where I'd managed to play it cool with Marco *all* day – what a miracle!) they made me put down my bags and get changed into an outfit Saff had created. It was my purple dress and black leggings, with a skinny ribbed cardie of hers and Grace's Converse. I have to admit, it looked pretty cool. Then Saff handed me my strappy handbag (lovely Mum had slipped a tenner in it for me, too), and they sent me downstairs. Mum was serious about doing a proper start-to-finish test run, so I was told to wait outside for a couple of minutes and then come in like an actual paying client.

The sign writer was up a ladder doing one of the final jobs – painting *Rainbow Beauty* in gorgeous purple curly lettering on a gold background above the door. That made it seem more really truly *real* to me than anything else we'd done so far, and I couldn't help smiling. It had just been an idea, a dream. Now it was actually happening and I was about to become the first customer. I carefully avoided walking under the ladder as I came in.

And there they all were, beaming at me.

Grace was on reception and she welcomed me and checked my appointment time on my little card, then invited me to take a seat on one of the purple velvet sofas (I was the first to be allowed to sit on one!). Then Saff came up, took my jacket, asked if I'd like tea or coffee and informed me that we had a selection of herbal teas too.

It was so funny, them pretending they didn't know me, and calling me *Madam* and stuff. Saff did my nails at the manicure station, and we couldn't help getting into hysterics when she asked me if I had any brothers or sisters and I made out like I had these two awful wicked older sisters, like Cinderella or something. Then she did my make-up while Mum whizzed up some delicious mango smoothies with apple juice, lime and honey in, and Grace set up one of the new CD players. She put on "Sisters Are Doin' It For Themselves" and soon we were all dancing round the shop, smoothies in hand, singing at the tops of our voices.

And then the phone rang.

I shimmied over to the reception desk and picked it up. "Good afternoon, Rainbow Beauty," I said in a posh telephone voice, and they all whooped and cheered.

"Abs? Is that you, love?"

My heart stopped. "Er, hello, Dad."

Mum, Saff and Grace fell silent. Grace ducked behind the desk, snapped off the music and then stormed out. Mum dashed after her.

"Are you okay, love? It's so good to speak to you," Dad was saying. "I've missed you girls so much, and I've been desperately worried about you all, but I didn't have a number for you till today. How is everything? Where are you? This is a Devon area code, isn't it? What on earth are you doing down there?"

"I, erm…" I stuttered. It was such a shock, and

too much to take in, and there was so much to say that I didn't know where to begin.

"Abs? Hon? Listen, love, this is a pay-as-you-go and I don't have much credit. Take the number down just in case I get cut off, could you?"

"Oh. Okay." I grabbed a scrap of paper and he gave me the number.

"Could you put Saff and Grace on too, love?" he said then.

I gestured at Saff to come to the phone but she shook her head. Then she stalked off after Grace and Mum.

"Erm, they aren't here," I mumbled.

"Oh, but they were a minute ago, I heard you all. Where have they gone? Don't they know I'm on the phone?"

Pause.

"Oh." He sighed. "But…you're my *daughters*."

You should have acted more like a father then, I thought but I bit my lip, then mumbled, "I'll get Mum."

"No, don't," he said quickly. "I'm not ready to speak to her."

"Well, I guess that's how Saff and Grace feel about you," I snapped. I couldn't help it, it just came out.

I winced as Dad made a sound like I'd punched

him in the stomach. "Well, so anyway, how have you been?" he asked again, trying to sound upbeat. "What's Rainbow Beauty?"

"It's our…business thing, this thing we're doing, with beauty stuff. We're opening a shop with…" But I couldn't get the words out. My head was all buzzy and my mouth didn't seem to be working properly. "It's the grand opening on Saturday and so we're—"

"Oh, wow, so soon? How did that happen? That's brilliant, good for you," he said. "I can't miss the big day. Listen, how about I try to borrow a mate's car and come down?"

I didn't say anything for a long time, but my brain was whizzing round and round, thinking, *How can I tell him not to come?* I was so confused, because on one hand I'd have loved him to be there for the opening, but on the other, I was furious – did he really think he could just rock up and expect us to welcome him with open arms? In the end I didn't have to speak. My silence said everything.

"I'll take that as a no then," he muttered. It sounded like he was going to cry at any minute. I felt the same.

"Dad, it's not that I don't want… It's just…"

He cleared his throat. "Look, you've obviously got a lot going on down there, so I'll leave you to it.

Good luck on Saturday, I hope it goes really well, and say hello to everyone from me." Pause. "I love you."

I tried to say it back, I really did, but the words just wouldn't come out, and then the line cut out and there was silence. "I love you too," I croaked, then put the phone down.

Suddenly I just felt so exhausted, like I wanted to lie down and sleep for a week.

They all piled back in then.

"He didn't want to speak to me, did he?" Mum cried. "What a coward!"

"How did he even get this number?" Saff demanded.

"I had to ring Roger and Laura about our stuff, so I asked them to pass it on, love," Mum explained.

"What?" Grace shrieked. "You *gave* it to him?"

Mum sighed. "Yes, and our address. He's your father, he has a right to know where you are."

"Well, he doesn't have a right to speak to me, not any more," Saff snarled. "After what he did, I never want to see him again!"

"I'm not speaking to him either," said Grace, "and you can tell him that if he calls again, Abbie. I don't care what he's got to say." Then she clenched her jaw and sank into a dark, brooding silence.

I felt terrible for Dad then. "Don't say that, he's

still our dad," I half-whispered, and they instantly jumped down my throat.

"Why are you defending him, after the way he's treated Mum?" Grace snapped.

"I'm not, I just—" I began, but Saff cut in.

"How can you be so calm about all this, Abs? It's like you're not even bothered by what he's done!"

I totally lost it then. All those times when they said I was the strong one? Well they were wrong.

"How dare you!" I shouted. "Course I'm bothered! It's there in my head *all the time*. I'd love to get really angry, like you, Saff, or have a good cry like Mum does, or be all superior like Grace – in fact I'd love to do *all* of that! But someone has to keep this family on track!"

They were just staring at me in stunned silence then.

"Abbie, love, I—" Mum began, but I wasn't finished. Not by a long way.

"It's *Dad* you're being so horrible to, you know!" I screamed. "The same Dad who bought that karaoke machine for you, Saff, when you were eight, and then sat through you giving whole concerts on it for the next four years, even though you can't sing for toffee!"

"How dare you, of course I can sing!" Saff

shrieked, but I ignored her and turned on Grace. "And it's the same Dad who hung that lantern on the wall outside your window," I shouted, "so you could see there were no monsters lurking in the garden at night. The same Dad who wrote that little letter for you to find in the bush, from the monsters, saying they'd gone to live somewhere else."

I fixed her, then Saff, with a piercing glare. "*Of course* he should have our number, and *of course* you two should talk to him. He was so upset when you wouldn't, and when he realized he wouldn't be welcome on Saturday—" My voice choked up in my throat then, and tears started sliding down my cheeks. "I mean, I don't think he should come either, it's too complicated, things are too…raw. But I'm just saying – he's *Dad*. He's our dad." Then the tears took over completely and I *had* to stop.

Saff looked really upset. "I wasn't being horrible to him. Well, I didn't *mean* to be."

"*I* did," said Grace coldly.

Mum put her arm round me. "Abbie, sweetheart, no one's being deliberately unkind," she said, glaring at Grace. "It's just, what happened was all such a shock and—"

"I know it was!" I sobbed. "I'm the one who's been there for you all, picking up the pieces, drying the tears, sorting out the problems." I looked at Saff and added, "Handing out the jelly babies. Basically, insisting that everything was going to be alright, even when I didn't believe it myself. Why do I always have to be the strong one? When do I get to have *my* meltdown?"

Mum looked horrified. "But Abbie, you know you can always talk—"

"No!" I shouted. "I don't want to talk about it! What's the point? What's happened has happened. I just wish you lot would realize that I'm no stronger than you are! I'm as hurt and scared and angry as the rest of you."

"Oh, Abs—" Saff cried. She tried to hug me, but I wriggled away. "I've got to go," I stuttered. "I've got a date, remember?" I was really crying by then, sobbing and choking on my words. I grabbed my strappy bag, marched to the door and stormed out.

Twenty minutes later, I couldn't believe I was actually there, in the cafe loos. What I'd felt like doing was running up to the flat, locking myself in my room (if I had one, ha ha, or any private space of my own, come to that), crying my eyes out for a very long time, then sleeping for even longer. But I was determined to carry on as usual. So there I was, trying to fix my make-up and get a smile to stay on my face. But it wasn't working and I had to keep pressing my lips together to keep from crying.

I still felt all trembly and sick and churned up inside when I walked out of the loos. Marco had arrived, and when he looked up and smiled at me my stomach did its familiar flip and I vowed not to let anything spoil this.

We hugged hello (cue even more stomach flipping) and Marco went up to the counter to get some drinks. I really tried to pull myself together then, but I couldn't – I just felt so miserable. He came back with strawberry milkshakes and handed me a menu. I held it up to my face and acted like I was really interested in reading about all the different kinds of burger, because I felt like if I started talking yet I'd just cry.

"Earth to Abbie – do you know what you want yet?" he said, grinning at me over the top of my menu. "For the third time of asking."

I realized I'd been staring blankly at the menu for ages, going over in my head what had happened back at Rainbow Beauty.

"Oh, sorry, erm, I don't know." I felt so sick and churny there was no way I'd be able to eat anything. "I mean, I'm not really hungry," I added lamely.

"Oh right," he said, giving me an intense look. I stared at the table, not wanting him to notice I'd been crying. Then he said, "If you don't fancy the food here we can go somewhere else."

"It's not that," I muttered. "I'm just not hungry. You go ahead though."

He shrugged. "Nah, you're alright. I'd feel funny eating on my own. I'll get something later."

"Oh, okay. How was band practice?" I managed to ask.

Luckily he got on to talking about that and didn't stop for ages and ages, and I could just nod occasionally. By then I'd realized that coming out was a total mistake, of course. I'd wanted him to see me as vibrant and witty and cool, but instead I felt small and washed-out and fragile, like I might shatter into a million pieces at any moment. The clatter and chatter around us was too loud for me, the lights were too bright, and suddenly...

I just had to get out of there.

I lurched to my feet, accidentally jogging the table and toppling my milkshake over. The glass hit the floor and smashed, and my drink splattered everywhere. And now noise wasn't a problem, because everyone was silent, staring at me.

Marco looked startled. And confused. "Oh, Abs,

it's okay," he said softly, seeing the shock on my face. Then, "Hey, where are you going?" he cried, as I turned and ran out onto the high street.

I wasn't sure where I *was* going at first, as I stumbled down the hill, but I did know I couldn't face the flat. Not yet anyway. I'd just decided to walk to Summer's when I saw a familiar face in a crowd of lads coming up the other side of the road.

Ben.

"Abbie!" he called, as they neared me, and then he instantly saw that I wasn't okay. He told his mates he'd catch them later and dashed across the road. Even though we were in the middle of the street, I couldn't help bursting into tears as I blurted out what had happened back at Rainbow Beauty.

He didn't say anything, apart from the occasional swear word. Instead, he just listened (and shuffled me over to sit on a shop window sill so a buggy could get past). And that's where I was, sitting on the ledge, drying my eyes on my sleeve, with Ben's arm round me, when Marco saw us.

He came marching up, looking furious. "Abbie! What's going on? Why did you just walk out like that? I felt like a total idiot!"

I couldn't believe it. He hadn't even noticed that I'd just been crying my eyes out!

"Well, now you know how it feels," I snapped.

"Oh, is that what all this was about, to get even after the gig?" he demanded. "Although why you were acting moody with *me* when it was you who went off with *him* for half an hour... Anyway, congratulations, you've made your point."

He was wrong, of course, but I couldn't be bothered to correct him.

"And now you two have met up to have a laugh about it!" he snarled.

"Mate——" Ben began.

"Mates don't steal girls off each other," Marco snapped.

"Excuse me, I'm not some kind of *object*!" I cried. "And anyway——"

"It's no big deal if you like Ben," Marco said coldly. "It's cool. Whatever. I just wish you'd been up front with me."

He was wrong again, but I didn't care – if he really thought I was horrible enough to lie about wanting to be friends, and then deliberately set him up to look stupid, and to go behind his back with his best mate... Well, if that was his opinion of me, he could get stuffed.

"Hang on, you don't——" Ben was saying, but Marco had already stormed off.

"He didn't even notice I was upset!" I fumed. "That might have given him *some* clue about why you had your arm round me. He thinks he can flirt with half the school but if I'm sat here with you, when we're so obviously just mates, he has a go at me! Idiot!"

I stood up, feeling the need to get moving again. But by then I'd realized that Summer's happy home was the last place I wanted to be.

"I'll walk with you," Ben offered.

I shook my head. "Thanks, but I'm not going back yet. I need some space."

"Okay," said Ben. "Look, it'll be alright, yeah?"

I managed a small smile. "See you later," I said.

"See you. Take care, okay?"

I headed towards Vire Island, totally ignoring the wolf whistles from the skateboarders I passed on The Plains. As soon as I crossed the little bridge onto the island, I felt calmer. I bought a coffee and some chocolate from the stand and sat on one of the benches right by the river. I didn't have any space of my own in the flat, so perhaps I could make this spot mine instead.

I sat there for ages, sipping my drink and thinking about Dad, and Marco, and Mum and my sisters. Then I watched the boats go by and tried not to think about anything at all. It did work, a bit, because after half an hour I felt slightly better. After another half an hour my bum started going numb and I got really hungry. So, even though the flat was the last place I wanted to be, I began wandering back.

I had a total shock when I got in – in a good way. Saff met me at the front door and put her hands over my eyes. I smelled paint, but I didn't guess what they were up to – I just thought it must be coming up from the shop.

"Saff, what are you doing?" I cried, as she walked behind me up the hall, pushing me along. She stopped and I felt Mum and Grace on either side of me.

"I know it's not easy, sharing a bedroom with your mother," Mum said, "especially as you've always liked your own space. I'm sorry there's no chance of a proper room of your own, but we hope this will help."

"Da daaa!" sang Grace, as Saff took her hands from my eyes.

I gasped, then giggled out in shock. Wow. I couldn't believe it. They'd turned the Hoover cupboard into a chill-out den for me. Mum had given the high window her cleaning treatment, so it seemed much lighter than before. The walls hummed with the warm glow of fairy lights against the burnt orange paint we hadn't been able to use downstairs. Two embroidered floor cushions lay on the leftover click-down laminate flooring. The CD player from one of the treatment rooms sat in the corner, with a stack of discs next to it.

"Do you like it?" squealed Saff, dancing about.

"I love it," I gasped. I reached out to touch the wall but, "Careful, it's still wet," Grace warned.

I drew my hand back and grinned at them all. "This is amazing. Thank you so much." Mum was right, I'd always used my room to dream and scheme, read, design beauty products, draw and write. I'd been really missing it, but I hadn't wanted to make a fuss – after all, no one else had their own space here. "Where did you get those?" I asked then, gesturing at the floor cushions.

"Liam's place," said Mum. "When I popped over to ask him if he'd come and put the flooring down, he said you could have them, because he was chucking them out anyway."

I felt a warm glow inside for him. I bet he hadn't really been throwing them away.

"We just want you to know we appreciate you so much," said Mum. She squeezed my shoulders and I leaned into her.

"I know," I said. "I'm sorry about losing it like that before."

"Don't be sorry," she said then. "You were right – we've all been so wrapped up in our own problems, and you always put such a positive spin on things… well, we didn't see that you were struggling too."

"We want to support you like you've supported us," said Grace.

"But you have to *let* us, Abs," Saff added.

I grinned at them. "Okay, point taken. But Saff, I didn't mean it about your singing." That wasn't exactly true – she was always breaking into song around the place, and to be honest she wasn't exactly Leona Lewis. But I never would have told her that if I hadn't been so upset. I had a feeling that Mum and Grace thought the same, but they hadn't said anything either. We all knew how important it was to Saff, and besides, who were we to say that she couldn't improve? So we were all really surprised when she just shrugged and said, "It's okay. I suppose I've always known deep down I'm not that good. But there are other things…acting, presenting… I'll get famous somehow."

None of us knew what to say then. "Oh, honey—" Mum finally began.

"It's fine. I'm fine, honestly," Saff insisted. "So

anyway, how was the date?" she asked me then.

"Oh, it didn't really happen in the end," I mumbled. "I just felt too…you know. Maybe another time."

"I'm sorry, hon," said Mum. "We ruined it for you, didn't we?"

"Dad did, you mean," Grace snapped.

I shrugged. "It was just bad timing, that's all." I didn't go into detail about what had happened. I couldn't go through all that drama with them again, not after the way they'd reacted when the gig thing went so badly. I'd learned my lesson about Marco now (finally), that was the main thing.

"Earlier, in the shop, you were wrong about one thing, though," Mum was saying. "It *is* worth talking things over, even if we can't change them. It *will* help you. Actually it'll help all of us. And because I know you find it hard to do, I've had an idea to help."

"Oh no, what are you planning now?" I grumbled, as they led me into the kitchen.

There were a few sheets of paper, some pens, a large saucepan and four glasses of water on the table. I just stared at them, with absolutely no idea what was going on.

"The pens and paper are for us to write down

what we wanted to say to Dad today, but didn't feel able to," Saff explained.

"Or didn't get the chance to, in my case," Mum grumbled.

"The pan is for us to burn them in, to let them go – is that right, Mum?" said Saff.

Mum nodded.

"And the glasses of water were my idea, in case the fire gets out of hand," said Grace.

"Good idea," I told her, "especially with me around."

They all grinned, remembering the setting-the-bathroom-alight episode.

"So, are you up for it?" asked Saff.

"Okay, fine," I said. So we all took a bit of paper and a pen and went to find a private corner of the flat to write. The paint was still wet in my chill-out room, so I sat on the bathroom floor and leaned against the bath to do mine.

When we came back together, there was a different atmosphere. The laughing and joking had stopped and we were all quiet and serious.

Mum lit the remains of my jasmine and bergamont candle and said, "Right, who wants to start?"

Unsurprisingly, Saff did.

I was expecting a furious tirade – I think we all

were – but instead she spoke in a small, trembling voice. "I can't believe it," she said simply. "I just can't believe you would do this to us. I keep thinking I'm going to wake up and it will all be a dream, and we'll be back home again, together. I just can't *believe* you could hurt us like this."

I should have realized before. Under all Saff's bolshiness and bluster she was just really, really hurt. Her trust in Dad had been shattered. She held her paper to the candle and when it blazed she threw it into the pan. Mum and I hugged her while Grace stood by with a glass of water in each hand, just in case.

"Well done, my darling angel," said Mum, which is what she used to call Saff when she was a little girl.

"Thanks," Saff half-whispered.

Grace suddenly picked up her paper and started reading then, and we all fell silent. "You really let us down, Dad," she said, in a sorrowful voice. "I trusted you to always look after us but you didn't and now I don't feel safe any more. I'm scared about everything – the present, the future, if school will be okay, if Rainbow Beauty will be okay, if *we'll* be okay." She trailed off, dissolving into tears, and for once she let us hug her, just for a moment, before setting light to her paper and throwing it into the pan.

"Your turn, Mum," said Saff.

Mum giggled a little hysterically. She pulled her bit of paper, well, *bits* of paper, from the pocket of her dress. They were completely covered in her big, loopy handwriting.

"Mum, that's an essay!" Grace teased.

"Think yourself lucky, if I'd had more time it would have been a novel," she muttered darkly. She took a deep breath and, clutching her words with trembling hands, she began. "How could you keep it from me, everything that was going on?" Pause. Deep breath. "We always tackled things together. Yes, of course I'm hurt about the affair and the business, but things like that aren't the end of the world. Together we could have sorted it out, and saved our family. Or even if we couldn't, we could have separated in a way which gave the girls more time to adjust. The thing that really cuts is that you didn't give me a chance to try and help fix things, you just vanished and left me to pick up the pieces."

Pause. Two deep breaths.

"When I married you I thought it was for ever. I knew there would be hard times – for richer, for poorer and all that. But when things got tough you just couldn't handle it. What a coward. And the worst thing is, you always said you'd give anyone hell who hurt our girls, but now you've hurt them more

233

than anyone else ever could. Luckily they're strong and sensible and we *will* get through this, but it didn't have to be this way, it really didn't." She breathed out sharply and screwed up her pages, then torched them with a look of satisfaction.

Everyone else had gone, so that made it my turn.

At first I didn't think I could do it, but when I glanced up to tell them that, their encouraging faces made me feel braver, and I started reading. "I do love you, Dad," I almost whispered. "I'm sorry I couldn't say it to you today, but I'm just so churned up and angry inside, and I feel like you don't deserve it. I feel sorry for you as well, but not too sorry – you've got a lot of making up to do. Look, I'm trying to feel better about everything, I just need more time." I glanced up. "Erm, that's it."

"Well done, Abbie," said Mum.

There were no tears – I think I'd done all my crying – but it felt good to say the things in my head out loud, and to be heard, even if it wasn't by Dad. At least he had our number now and I had his. I promised myself that when things had calmed down a bit, I'd call him and say some of these things actually *to* him. Maybe some of the angry and hurt bits. Definitely the *I love you* part.

I burned my paper and we all had a big hug,

pulling Grace in whether she liked it or not.

When we finally broke apart, Mum said, "Right! Good! Now we're all going to cheer up, because it's a *good* thing that we're moving on with our lives – as much as we can for now, anyway. And that's why...ta daa!" She opened the fridge and revealed all this lovely food.

"Wow, Mum, this is amazing!" I gasped, as Saff began passing it out onto the table.

"Oh, it's nothing, just some little nibbles I put together for the launch," Mum insisted, as the table filled with plate after plate of aromatic colourful deliciousness. "I thought I should try the combinations out on you lot first – I don't want to go putting our clients off."

Of course there was no chance of that. Mum's been making canapés for years for her dinner parties and summer cocktail evenings, and she's brilliant at it. She just knew we needed a boost.

There were mini quiches with asparagus and Gruyère, goat's-cheese-and-redcurrant-chutney crostini, and strips of smoked salmon wrapped around cream cheese. She'd filled vol-au-vent cases, some with prawn mousse with shrimps on top, and some with pepperonata, mozzarella and olives. She'd made sweet treats too – rainbow fruit salad sticks made of strawberries, blueberries, papaya and pineapple pieces, with a little pot of vanilla cream to dip them into.

"Can we afford to eat these now, though?" asked Grace, frowning. "Maybe we should save them for Saturday, rather than making a new lot. Every penny has to go into the business, remember?"

Mum grinned. "These didn't come out of our budget. Listen, girls – they can take our house, our car, our possessions, even the shirts off our backs, but they can't take our Nectar points! Turns out I'd saved up more than enough to treat you all, so I took the bus to the Sainsbury's in Paignton."

So we sat down to the lovely feast, laughing and joking, talking about all our plans and arrangements for the grand opening.

"Oh, and what did Roger and Laura say about our stuff?" Grace asked, through a mouthful of vol-au-vent.

Mum frowned. "Not great news, I'm afraid. By the time they got round there, the bailiffs were already taking all the electrical goods, and the rest of my shoes, and our figurines. But when they'd gone, Roger and Laura went in and cleared out everything else and it's in their garage waiting for us. The main thing is, we didn't lose anything that really matters.

We've still got the big scrapbook of pictures you did in primary school, and all the boxes of birthday and Christmas cards. They didn't touch Great-Grandpa Green's war medals and papers, thank goodness, and the family photos weren't taken."

"And pink rabbit?" I asked. He was only a tatty old pyjama case, but I loved him.

Mum nodded. "Yep, safe and sound. And blue bear," she added, winking at Grace. Grace couldn't help smiling, even though she'd announced three years ago that she was far too old for blue bear and shoved him in the back of her wardrobe.

"And my hair tongs?" asked Saff anxiously. "*Please* say they left those."

We all burst out laughing at that.

"What?!" she demanded. "I really love them, okay?"

Saying those things to Dad, even though he couldn't hear us, well, it was like a weight had lifted off our shoulders. As the table glistened with the beautiful, fresh, scrumptious treats, even the air around us felt lighter and more sparkly somehow. It really did feel like a proper new start. Not like we were running away from our old life any more, but like we were running towards a new one.

Chapter Twelve

Marco wasn't speaking to me on Friday at school, which was fine by me, because I wasn't speaking to him either. At least it was the last day of term, so once it was over I wouldn't be forced to look at him all day long. Summer asked what was going on a couple of times, but I just said I didn't want to go into it. I was too busy thinking about the grand opening of Rainbow Beauty, and all the little things we still had to finish off. "Let's just say he had his last chance, and he blew it," I mumbled, then went all businesslike and marched her off to the library to finish the last few sheets of product labels.

After school, Grace and I hurried back to the

shop so we could help put the final bits and pieces in place. So at half six, Grace was giving the floor a sweep and mop and Saff and Mum were arranging the vases of flowers. As I tipped my free sample lip balms into a basket on the reception desk, a knock on the window made all of us look up.

It was Marco.

For a moment I thought about stropping off into the kitchenette and refusing to see him. But I knew we had to sort things out, for Summer and Ben's sakes if nothing else. Because of us fighting, they'd had a rubbish day too. And poor Ben had given up trying to convince Marco that there was nothing going on between us two. So I took a deep breath, tried to stop my legs from shaking and strode out of the shop.

I automatically walked right up close to him, and I had to make myself take a step back. My stomach did its familiar flip as I took in his gorgeousness, but then I got a grip on myself. "Hi," I mumbled.

"Hi."

Cue a long, agonizing silence. *He's come to me,* I thought. *He can speak first.*

He looked really uncomfortable, his hands shoved into his pockets, swaying from foot to foot. "I, erm, I just thought maybe…I'm guessing you won't want me here tomorrow, so I came to say, you know, erm, good luck and that."

Right. So no apology then.

"It's cool if you're with Ben," he said then. "He's a really good bloke. I shouldn't have been an idiot about it. It's not like me and you were together or anything."

I sighed. Not this again. "Oh my God, how many times? There is *nothing* going on with Ben," I insisted. "I don't fancy him. *Not* that I have to explain myself to you," I added, scowling at him.

He gave me a playful look. "So, have you totally gone off me now, then?"

Argh, he was just so full of himself! I was going to tell him to get lost then (or get Saff to come out and say it with wellies) but I remembered how much better I'd felt after being honest about my feelings when we did the burning pot thing. I decided it was time to tell Marco how I really felt about what had happened between us, even if it did make me seem uptight and uncool.

"If you'd actually *looked* instead of going off on one yesterday, you'd have noticed that Ben had his arm round me because I was *upset*," I said. Marco looked genuinely surprised at that. Still, I pushed on. "And, do you really think I was just setting you up in

240

the cafe? To make you feel stupid like I felt at the gig? Is that what you actually think I'm *like*?"

"Of course not," he insisted. "I didn't mean that. I wasn't thinking straight. I just felt such an idiot and I didn't know why you'd been so weird with me and then run off, and when I saw you with Ben I just assumed—"

"Well, you were wrong," I snapped. "Not everything's about *you*, you know." Then I told him about Dad's call, and my family's reaction, and my major meltdown.

I was half expecting him to make some lame excuse to do a runner then. After all, I probably sounded like I had some serious *issues*. But he just listened, looking really shocked. "But why didn't you tell me about it as soon as I got to the cafe?" he asked. "I was right there in front of you. How come you talked to Ben and not me?"

"Okay, I'm sorry," I conceded. "I shouldn't have tried to hide being upset. The truth is, I can talk to Ben because he *is* just a mate. But with you, well…" I steeled myself. I knew it was going to be embarrassing to admit this, but it had to be said. "I wanted to impress you. I wanted you to see me as happy and bubbly. I wanted to be the cool girl you think I am, not the scared, broken one who feels

241

like she'll never be properly happy again."

He blinked at me. "I don't think you're one girl or another girl. I think you're you. But I know what you mean – I wanted to impress you too."

Well, that annoyed me. "Yeah, *right*. If you're so into me, why did you ask me to the gig then act like I wasn't there?" I demanded.

He looked confused. "What?"

"Oh, come on," I snapped. "You know what I'm talking about. It's lucky Ben *was* there, and Summer, otherwise I'd've been standing on my own while my so-called *date* flirted with that group of girls."

He sighed. "Oh God. And you thought… No… I was only talking to them because I wanted to impress you, for you to think I was popular… I realize how lame that sounds now. Oh, jeez, I really have messed this up, haven't I? Honestly, I was just coming over to be with you and you walked out. You were gone for ages, with Ben, and I thought you were playing games with me. Playing us off against each other."

I sighed. "For goodness' sake, when are you going to realize I'm not *like* that?!"

"I know. I'm sorry. I wasn't thinking straight." He looked right into my eyes, then glanced away. But I'd seen it. He really was embarrassed, and ashamed.

"It's no excuse, but you kind of make my brain go mushy," he said then. "Well, *more* mushy."

I thought back to the potassium-chlorate-and-fourteen-gummy-bears disaster. I had to admit I knew what he meant. Still, I wasn't letting him off that easily. "You had loads of chances to speak to me," I pointed out. "I came over and stood next to you for about *fifteen minutes*, but you just acted like I wasn't there. You didn't even introduce me to the band."

"I know how it looks, but honestly, I was just about to, but then... I could see they were all wowed by you – you looked so stunning, and well... Declan has a great voice, and Tay's such a talented songwriter. Chaz is just totally cool. How long would it have been before you decided you'd rather be with one of them instead?"

"That's so stupid!" I cried. "How shallow do you think I am? I went there with *you* because I really liked *you*."

"*Liked*, past tense?" he asked.

I didn't say anything.

He sighed. "Look, everything you've said about me is true. I was so keen to impress you that I've ended up doing the complete opposite. And I've totally misjudged you – more than once. I've been an idiot, I know. But the thing is, I wanted to be with you from the first moment we met in that storm. Right from then, I couldn't think about anyone else. I've never felt like this about anyone before and I didn't know how to handle it. And now I've made a total mess of everything."

He took my hand. Electricity crackled between us like it did on that first day. It took me right back there. Yes, he'd misjudged me, but I'd got him wrong too. I'd only seen his vain, arrogant façade, and not the tangle of feelings that were hiding underneath.

"Please, Abbie, give me another chance."

I looked right into his eyes then, and I knew he was telling the truth about how he felt. It was what I'd always wanted. Always hoped for.

But I shook my head.

"I can't," I told him. The words stuck in my throat but I made myself say them. "I know now that you didn't mean to mess stuff up, and I promise you, I didn't either. But every time we try to get together, it ends in disaster. And there's just so much going on in my life right now that if it went wrong again, well, I don't think I could deal with it."

I forced myself to pull my hand away.

He was just staring at me — he looked gutted, and I felt awful too, like there was a big rock in my stomach. I didn't think I could bear it, but then I told myself to be strong. I'd had my heart ripped out once by Dad – if Marco did that to me too, I knew I wouldn't be able to handle it. I needed to keep my head and focus on making the business work, for my family's sake.

"I've blown it, haven't I?" he said finally.

"It's not you," I insisted. "Well, not just you. It's bad timing, mainly. Look, please can we stay friends? I love hanging out with you guys. It was awful today, for all of us. I don't want it to be like that."

I braced myself, expecting him to tell me where I could put my friendship. I knew how proud he was, and I'd just knocked him back. But, "Okay," he said. "Friends is okay, I guess."

And then he just walked away, without saying goodbye. And I felt like my heart had gone with him, but I didn't call him back.

When I got back upstairs, Mum was making a new batch of scrummy canapés for the launch (and this time slapping our hands away if we tried to pinch any). Saff and Grace were piling products into boxes to take downstairs. I said hi and started getting the stuff out to make my final two fresh face masks.

"Well?" Saff demanded. Mum and Grace were giving me eager looks too.

"Well what?" I mumbled. But I knew there was no way they were going to let me get away without telling them what had happened with Marco. In fact, I was amazed they'd managed not to stick their ears up to the front window. I told them almost word for word what we'd said (Grace had insisted on the *exact* detail), then…

"Oh, that's dead romantic!" cried Saff. "Love at first sight, just like Romeo and Juliet."

"*Dead* romantic is right," Grace snorted. "Romeo and Juliet both snuffed it."

Saff glared at her. "You always have to spoil it, don't you?"

"It *is* all a bit Elizabeth Bennett and Mr. Darcy," said Mum dreamily.

"Aren't they the ones from that old TV series you've watched about a million times?" Saff asked her. "Where that fit guy comes out of the lake in that wet shirt?"

Mum nodded, with a faraway look on her face.

"It was a book first, you idiot," Grace snapped. "*Pride and Prejudice*? Does that ring any bells? You just did it for GCSE English!"

But Saff didn't snap back. She'd joined Mum in

her Mr. Darcy-induced trance.

"Erm, hello?!" I cried. "Didn't *any* of you hear *anything* I just said? We're not *getting* together. I told him it was over, whatever *it* was in the first place. We're just going to be friends."

"Oh, right," said Mum, coming to. She put her arm around me. "Are you okay, hon?"

I shrugged. "Yes. No. I don't know."

Saff looked about four years old then, clutching Grace's arm. "But you will get together in the end, won't you?" she gasped, wide-eyed.

"Get real, Saff," Grace snapped. "Life's not like a fairy tale."

"Do you want to talk about it?" Mum asked me.

I shook my head. There was nothing left to say, so I just sighed loudly, put on my apron, gloves and attractive hairnet, and got on with measuring out the blueberries.

Chapter Thirteen

On the morning of the grand opening, we all got dressed in our pink uniforms and did our hair and make-up. Even Grace put on a bit of mascara and let Saff style her hair. Then Mum handed out the name badges she'd ordered for us. My heart was pounding as I pinned mine on – this really was IT.

"Ready?" she asked us, looking as nervous as I felt.

"Ready," we replied, and we all filed downstairs.

When we'd finally finished everything down here the night before (long after I'd done the face masks) we'd just been so tired, we'd stumbled straight up to bed. We hadn't looked...well, not *really* looked.

But now, as we stepped through the door of Rainbow Beauty, we couldn't help gasping in sheer amazement. Sun was streaming through the window and across the glossy floor. The old gold paint effect on the reception desk worked really well, and the vase of bright flowers brought the whole area to life. Our slogan sang out, stencilled onto the wall behind it: *Rainbow Beauty – beauty from the inside out.*

The sofa area with its coffee table and magazines was so inviting. The chiller counter was full of bright, glistening fresh fruit, which looked delicious, and made a great backdrop for the little tubs of fresh face mask nestled amongst it. In a squealing huddle we bounced over to the treatment rooms. They were cosy havens with low light, delicious-smelling oil diffusers and big fluffy towels ready at the foot of each massage table.

It was just like I'd dreamed it – only better.

Mum took my hand, and Saff's on the other side, and Saff grabbed Grace's and we all stood there for a moment, beaming at each other.

Then Summer walked in, gabbling on about how fab it all looked, followed by Liam, who looked like he needed to sleep for a week. After all the hellos, Mum leaped into action, sending Saff and Grace back upstairs for the food, asking Liam to sort out a sticking door, and telling me and Summer to get the kettle on for teas all round.

As we stood in the tiny kitchenette, I told Summer about Marco coming over, and that we'd made up, but how we were just going to be friends. "I've always been really into him," I admitted, "and now I know he's really into me too. But I've decided it's not going to happen. We'd only mess it up again, and I can't risk wrecking our group. I love us all hanging out together."

Summer peered at me. "Are you sure?" she asked.

"Yes," I said firmly.

She sighed. "Well, it's probably for the best."

"Yes, it is."

Just then Marco appeared in the doorway and we both looked so flustered, it must have been obvious we'd been talking about him. He grinned, a little nervously. "Erm, hi. Should I go out and come back in again?"

"Course not. We weren't talking about you or anything," I gabbled. "Erm, Summer was just telling me about this exercise I can do to help my…" (Think, Abbie, think!) "…terrible period pain." (Yikes! Where did that come from?!)

He looked even more awkward then. "Oh. Er, right. I'll leave you to it, in that case."

Every time I looked at him after that I wanted to die of embarrassment. *Period exercises?* Argh! Why couldn't I just say anything *normal* around him?

But soon I had something far more serious to worry about. We all did.

With a noisy countdown and a big cheer, we opened the doors at ten o'clock on the dot. And okay, so no one was waiting outside or anything, but we thought they'd start to trickle in a few minutes later. But by half past, there was still no sign of anyone and I was starting to get a horrible sick feeling in my stomach.

Soon, Mum was peering at one of my leaflets. "I'm just double-checking these do say *ten* o'clock," she said. "Ah. Here. Yes, of course they do. Sorry, Abbie. I just thought maybe..."

"No one ever comes to this kind of thing right on time," Liam reassured her. "Don't worry, they'll be along soon."

But as the clock ticked towards eleven, even he had to admit it wasn't looking good. Mum's brave face slipped first. "I can't believe this is happening," she said shakily. "I mean, look at everything we've done... All the love, the care, the hard work. All the faith. What if it's been for nothing?"

I glanced from her sorrowful face to her lovingly-arranged plates of canapés and back, and thought my heart would burst.

Liam wrapped her up in a hug, but no one spoke. We all felt it – that horrible feeling that we'd done all this and no one cared. No one was interested. I felt Summer's arm round my shoulders, and that made me feel like crying too.

The door opened and we all glanced up. But it was only Ben. He breezed in, saying, "Hi all, sorry I'm late, Mum was having a nightmare with Gabe so I stayed to…" Then he trailed off, noticing the obvious. "Erm, where is everybody?"

"No one's——" I began, but just then, the door opened again and this time an actual customer walked in. We were all so shocked, we ended up just staring at her in silence. To be honest, I wouldn't have blamed her if she'd run back out again. But then Mum smiled and smoothed down her uniform and went over to greet her.

Grace offered her a juice and some canapés, Saff showed her the treatment rooms, and Mum talked her through the treatments we had on offer. When I gave her a sample lip balm, she took the lid off and had a sniff straight away. "Mmm, this smells delicious," she enthused. "And the whole place is beautiful. It's just what we need at this end of town, it'll really give the parade a lift." Then she added, "It's a shame you picked today to launch, though."

We all looked at her, puzzled. "How do you mean?" Mum asked.

She looked surprised. "Oh, didn't you know? It's the big arts and crafts fayre in Borough Park today. It's only once a year and they've been advertising it for weeks. There are over a hundred stalls and a band, food... Everyone will be up there this morning. I'm on my way now, actually."

Mum frowned. "Oh, right. No, we didn't know."

We all had to smile and say goodbye nicely of course, but as soon as she'd left we broke out into dismayed chatter.

"I can't believe we missed something so obvious!" Mum cried.

"I feel terrible," said Summer. "They have this every year, but I just didn't click that it was the same date."

"It's my fault," Liam insisted. "I even saw a poster for it. I should have put two and two together."

"I knew it was happening," said Ben, "but I've never been, so I didn't realize it was such a big deal."

"Emily mentioned it to me," said Saff, "but in Ealing there are loads of events going on at the same time, so I didn't think it would matter."

Grace, of course, hadn't known anything about it. And nor had I.

I felt as sick as everyone else looked. But I knew there was no point sitting round blaming ourselves. "The important thing is, what can we do about it now?" I asked.

And before anyone could say anything, a solution flashed into my mind. Mum and I looked at each other, and I knew she'd had the same idea. "Well, if Mohammed won't come to the mountain, the mountain must go to Mohammed," she said.

"Say what?" asked Saff.

Grace rolled her eyes. "She means, we're the mountain, and the clients are Mohammed."

Saff frowned. "I still don't get you."

Grace sighed. "If they're not coming to us, we'll go to them, duh!"

"Oh right," Saff snapped. "Why didn't you just say so? But hang on, what if they don't let us in?"

Mum just looked really determined. "I'll persuade them to make room for us," she said, with that old glint of steel in her eye.

So it was all hands on deck then, to pack up most of the food and samples and leaflets and products into Liam's van. We also took his long wallpaper-pasting table and three huge fluffy pink towels to cover it, in case there was room for us to set it up.

Saff's friend Emily arrived just as we were about to head off, and we couldn't believe it – she was such a total clone of Saff, *they* could have been the sisters. Typical boys, Ben and Marco couldn't stop staring at her, and you could see them thinking, *Wow, there are two of them!* I had to snap my fingers in front of their faces in the end and say, "Can we focus, please?"

It was decided that Emily, Summer and the boys would stay at the shop, and Mum would drive me, Saff and Grace up to the fayre in Liam's van. Emily would do a head massage demo on anyone who did come in, and Summer could handle the free nail painting. Ben was in charge of making smoothies and juices, and Liam was just in charge full stop. Marco offered to go down to the junction with more leaflets and stop people on their way to the fayre to invite them to pop in to Rainbow Beauty first, or to look out for us when they got there. "I'm sure I can get loads of people in," he said. Then he smiled sadly at me and added, "Luckily not *everyone*'s immune to my charms."

Just as we were all in the van about to set off, Liam leaned in to the driver's side window and asked Mum if she had her phone with her. "No, it's up in the flat," she said, looking confused.

"Here, take my mobile," he said, passing it through the window. "You'll need to call us when people make appointments, and then I can write them straight in the book, so we don't double-book anything."

Mum hesitated. "I'm not sure whether anyone will book in on the spot."

Liam grinned at her. "Think positive, Kim. Come on, you've got this far on passion and guts. Don't lose faith now."

Mum grinned back, then turned to us. "Come on, girls, let's get out there and show the world what we're made of."

"Yeah!" we all cried, whooping and cheering.

And with that she started the van, stalled it, started it again, bunny-hopped down the road with the handbrake on for a bit, then finally we were off. I turned to wave and couldn't help giggling when I saw Liam with his head in his hands.

Two wrong turns and one more stall in the middle of a junction later, we arrived at Borough Park. Luckily when we explained our situation, the lady at the gate was really nice and squeezed us in next to a lighting company's stand. The fayre was in full swing, with a really buzzy atmosphere, a band playing, food and drink stands and loads of cool stalls. There were crystals, wicker baskets, pottery, handmade wooden toys and games, and I spotted this fab stall selling bags made out of recycled sweet packets.

Not that I had time to go over for a look. We set everything up at lightning speed and even as we were still laying things out, people started to crowd around and pick up the products for a sniff, or to look at the ingredients lists. They seemed to be really pleased about the fact that everything was fresh and natural, and I was soon chatting away, giving loads of information on where the different ingredients had come from, and which were certified organic, and exactly how long the different fresh face masks would last in the fridge and…well, everything! It was brilliant getting to talk about what I really loved and the products were just flying off the table. Mum took the money for me, putting the things in our special recycled paper bags and writing out receipts.

When I had a minute's break, I noticed that Grace had propped up a sign next to the free sample lip balms. Well, they weren't free any more. *Free lip balm when you book a treatment today*, the sign read. I don't know whether it made any difference, but people were certainly booking up – Saff was talking them through the choices, or they were taking our list away to look at and then popping back to book in. Mum definitely needed Liam's mobile – she was on it about every five minutes. And she reported back to us that they'd had quite a few people going into Rainbow Beauty in the end too, thanks to Marco's efforts.

Summer's friends Iola and Amany from Art Club came up and said hi (and bought some Avocado Body Butter). Olivia and Rose from netball were there with Rachel, Jess and Bex from our year too. They came over to chat and ended up booking themselves in all together for manicures next Saturday. Some people came over who seemed to know Mum, and she told us they were from one of the hotels she'd been into to ask about jobs. They took some of our cards and promised to send their guests our way for treatments, as they didn't offer any themselves.

Saff got chatting to a group of second years from the course she'd (hopefully) be doing, and they were all asking about work placements. Mum took their details and said she'd keep them posted, as it might not be long before we needed some extra help (positive thinking again!). Grace's new friends came over and had a chat with her, and afterwards Mum, me and Saff couldn't resist teasing her a bit because Aran, her mate from Extended Maths, *so* obviously fancied her. She just told us all not to be silly, of course, but then she blushed bright red, grabbed a pile of leaflets and rushed off, saying she was going to give them out round the fayre.

We just enjoyed the whole thing so much. When it quietened down, and we'd very nearly sold out of products, we got to have a look round the other stalls, too. Of course, we were under strict instructions from Mum not to spend all the profit we'd made, but we took a few of the little cards for a handmade jewellery store and a candle shop to put on our reception desk and they took some of ours to put by their tills, and while we were there I swapped some bath bombs for a really cool pyramid candle.

We got back to Rainbow Beauty on a total high, dancing through the door whooping and cheering (until Liam noticed his van inching its way back down the road and Mum had to rush out to put the handbrake *on* this time). Over tea and leftover canapés in the sunshine out the front, we worked out that altogether we'd made £384 on the product sales. Grace said that more than covered our whole ingredients spend on the first batch, and there was still a bit of stock left on the shelves, too.

Between our bookings and Liam's, we were full for most of the week ahead and half the week after. Summer told us that her mum and dad had been in too, and bought two of the Carrot & Calendula Hand Balms Annie had inspired me to create. Summer said they'd been sorry not to see us all, but that Annie had booked in for a massage, so they'd get to meet her soon.

"And I'm treating my mum to something," said Ben. "She deserves it with Gabe's teething trouble. I'm going to take the treatment list home so she can choose."

"Wow, Ben, that's really nice of you, love," said Mum. "And so good of you all to help out. A toast," she announced, raising her mug, "to Liam, Summer, Ben, Marco and Emily. Thanks for everything. Really, you don't know how much your support means to us."

"Cheers!" I said quickly, because it looked like she might burst into tears again.

"Cheers!" everyone cried, and we all clinked our mugs together.

The group started to break up soon after. Ben had to get home to help out with Gabe, and Summer had her usual Saturday night family meal to get back for. Mum was off to the local for a drink with Liam, and Saff was heading back into town with Emily. She did ask Grace and me along, which was really nice of her, but Grace said she was going to curl up in their room with her Extended Maths workbook and I said I'd stay down in Rainbow Beauty and get everything tidied up.

As everyone milled around, saying goodbyes and getting their stuff together, I found myself standing with Marco.

"Well, thanks for today," I said.

He grinned. "You already thanked me. Twice."

"Oh, okay. Well, I guess I'll say bye then."

"Okay, well, bye then."

Yikes! Massivo awkwardness alert! First we didn't know what to do and we just sort of hovered there in embarrassed silence. In the end he went in for a hug, but I thought he was doing the kissing-on-two-cheeks thing instead, so we ended up banging heads.

"Ow!" I cried.

"Oh, God, sorry," he mumbled.

"No, *I'm* sorry. Are you okay?" I asked.

He smiled. "I've survived worse. Being viciously stabbed in the hand with a glass rod, for example."

I grimaced. "Oh God, I'd forgotten about that. This isn't my violent streak coming out again, I promise."

Violent streak? What was I even *on* about? Then, just when I thought it couldn't get any more awkward, I found myself holding out my hand for him to shake. CRINGE! Where on earth had that come from? I'd done the same stupid thing that first time we met too. *No, Abbie,* I told myself sternly. *Don't think about that day.*

Still, even if he did think I was a total dork, he just gave me an amused smile and shook it.

"Okay, bye, see ya," I muttered, forcing myself to let go of his hand.

"Yeah, see ya." And then he went striding along the pavement to catch up with Ben.

For a moment there I'd thought he was going to say something. I mean, *really* say something. You know, about me and him. And I realized then what I guess I'd known deep down all along.

That I wanted him to.

But it was too late now. I'd blown it.

I'd turned him down and he wasn't going to beg. His pride wouldn't stand for it. And I wasn't going to chase him any more. If he wasn't going to make a move then nor was I.

So I guess that really was IT.

I was still down in Rainbow Beauty a couple of hours later, pottering around, when I found the card. I was going through the post – no one had had time to open it with so much going on – and I saw it. *The*

Greens it said, instead of one name. And inside there were two words, in Dad's scribbly handwriting: *Good luck*. And four kisses. I sighed and hugged it to my chest for a while, then I put it up on the reception desk. I didn't think anyone else would want to see it, but I wasn't going to hide it from them.

I gave the floor another sweep, then arranged the stock on the shelves and made a list of which ingredients we'd need to buy more of for the next batch. After that, I checked that the scrap of paper with Dad's number on was still tucked into the back of the appointments book. I didn't want to ring him, not right now, but it was good to know it was there. Then I washed up the smoothie glasses and canapé plates in the little kitchenette, and I was just drying them up when the CD player behind the reception desk came on.

I froze for a moment, listening. It was Judy Garland, singing "Somewhere over the Rainbow".

Mum had got back from the pub half an hour before, so I assumed she'd popped down to see what I was up to and put it on.

"Hi, Mum," I called, as I headed back into the shop. "I've just done a stocktake and—"

I stopped still. It wasn't Mum.

It was Marco.

"Erm, hi…again," he mumbled.

"Hi." My stomach did its familiar flip. It just felt so good to be near him, so *right*. I tried to pull the washing-up gloves off really quickly and ended up with my hand stuck and the fingers stretching longer and longer. Then – YIKES – I actually *grunted* with the effort, then the glove pinged off and slapped me in the face. "OW!" I yelled. *All hail Abbie Green, queen of sophistication.*

"Are you okay?" he asked. The way I was acting, he probably meant *in the head*.

I blushed, mumbled, "Yeah, fine," and wrestled off the other glove. When I finally glanced back up at him, I saw that he looked really serious.

"I came back to say, I can't be friends with you," he said.

My stomach flipped again, but not in a good way this time. "Why not?" I stuttered. "I thought we agreed—"

He grimaced. "Well, I've been thinking about it and it seems like a very bad idea. You'll always be telling me about your period exercises and stuff…" He gave me a nervous smile. "I think it's much better if we're *more* than friends."

My heart started pounding. Was this really happening?

I raised my eyebrows. "Oh, you think so, do you?"

"Look," he said, suddenly serious again. "I get what you said about having a lot on your plate right now, and it's fine if you do just want to be friends. Well, it's not, actually. I don't know if I could even be around you just as friends, but I'll try if that's what you want. But so there's no more confusion, I want you to know where I stand. I want to be with you. I want you to be my girlfriend. I'll be a good thing in your life. I won't make things harder for you, and if I do, ever, you know you can tell me. You can tell me anything. Please, *please* give me another chance, Abbie."

OMG, so he actually *was* begging.

I looked at him for a moment, trying to weigh everything up in my mind — all that had happened, all that might happen, how good it could be, how badly wrong it could go, whether I was even ready to see anyone. I really didn't know what the answer was. But then my heart took over and I just said, "Yes."

"What, really?" He looked startled.

I giggled. "Yes."

"Phew! Thank God for that!" He smiled his beautiful, slow, knowing smile. "Dance with me," he said, pulling me into his arms.

This time I let myself move in close to him and

breathe in his cinnamon and musk swirl. That lightning crackle buzzed between us as I put my arms around his neck. Then I realized that dancing should probably involve moving your feet, but when I tried they seemed to be stuck to the ground, so I just kind of swayed from side to side.

And as Judy sang about bluebirds and lemon drops and making dreams come true, he kissed me. And I kissed him back, a perfect, lip balmy, Peppermint Kiss.

When he'd gone, I stood in the exact same spot for a while, replaying every word, look, touch…and that kiss, of course. I wanted it all to be there, safe in my memory, till I was so old I wore flapping nun-thickness tights out of *choice*.

Finally I locked up and headed upstairs. Mum and Grace were in the kitchen, and Saff came out of the bathroom in her dressing gown just as I walked in. When she saw the mile-wide grin on my face, she just squealed and started dancing about. "Ooooooh! He came back, didn't he?"

I nodded.

She let out an ear-splitting scream. "Yes, I knew it! I knew it!"

"Who, Liam? What for?" asked Grace, looking puzzled, and making us all burst out laughing.

"You don't understand anything, do you, Grace?" Saff teased.

But instead of being offended, Grace just grinned. "Only kidding. I know you mean Marco. I'm really happy for you, Abs."

Saff gave her a smug look. "See? Life *can* be a fairy tale – if you believe it can."

"Well, this, and everything else that's happened today, definitely calls for a celebration!" Mum announced. So she went and got the juicer from downstairs and whizzed up something special for us with pineapple, strawberries and blueberries in. Meanwhile, Grace got the CD player from my chill-out room and Saff disappeared to their room for a while and returned in a spangly minidress with a stack of CDs.

"I know the perfect song for us," she said, putting on "Higher" by The Saturdays.

Mum handed out the smoothies. "To Rainbow Beauty," she said, raising her glass.

"To Rainbow Beauty," we chanted, clinking our drinks together.

And then, "To Abbie," she added, "who kept us together and lifted us higher."

"To Abbie," echoed Saff and Grace, clinking glasses with me again.

Then, "Speech!" Grace cried.

I smiled, but shook my head. I didn't think there was anything I wanted to say. But then I realized there was, which was lucky, because my sisters had set up a chorus of "Speech, speech, speech, speech, speech!"

"Alright!" I shouted, over the music and their din. "Okay, well, Mum, it was that night you talked about selling your ring that it really hit me. I felt like we'd lost not just our house, but our *home*. But I was wrong about that. Because I know now that home is wherever you all are. I'm so proud of us. We've been through a hard time, but we've picked ourselves up and made sure something good's come out of it. We've made our dream of opening Rainbow Beauty come true."

"And you've found your dream boy!" Saff cut in. They all whooped and cheered, making me blush the colour of Mum's special celebration smoothie.

I grinned. "And best of all," I added, "this is just the beginning."

School's out for the summer holidays,
and there's no stopping Abbie at

Rainbow Beauty

Turn the page for a sneak preview of
the next gorgeous book

Strawberry
Summer

Chapter One

"Abbie, love, have you got the things we need for Mrs. Smith?" said Mum. "It's a full body massage and facial."

"I know. Just sorting it," I replied.

I hurried over to one of our treatment rooms, a pot of Blueberry Burst Fresh Face Mask in one hand (my very own secret recipe), and a bottle of Uplifting Rose and Geranium Oil in the other. I folded some towels neatly on the couch and arranged the products on top of them. Then I lit the oil burner to fill the air with the scents of jasmine and ylang ylang and put on some relaxing music, ready for our first client who was due any minute.

Looking around, I could still hardly believe we'd made all this happen. Every single bit of Rainbow Beauty was absolutely gorgeous. I loved the squishy purple velvet sofas and old gold-painted reception desk, with its vase of pink roses. The marble smoothie bar with its retro stools was so cool, and the chiller counter looked delicious, with little tubs of face mask arranged amongst the fresh blueberries, mangoes, passion fruits, pears, lemons and strawberries. I loved the glass shelves with all our natural, handmade products displayed on them too, like magic potions, waiting for you to pick the perfect one to cheer you up, or calm you down, or make you feel like you could take on the world – and make it your own.

We had quite a few bookings. I guessed lots of people wanted to get themselves looking their best before going on holiday. The bell over the door jangled as Mrs. Smith came in. Mum smoothed down her pink uniform and welcomed her, smiling warmly.

My sisters were on hand too – Grace took her jacket while Saff asked if she'd like one of our fresh juices or smoothies. She chose an immune-boosting green one from the menu (it included spinach and stinging nettles, but tasted really yummy – yes, honestly!). I made it for her then Mum led her into the gorgeous oasis of the treatment room.

An hour later she emerged walking on air, and saying how much she'd enjoyed it. She ended up staying for a manicure with Saff and when that was finished, she bought a bag of Lavender Bath Bombs and a pot of Carrot & Calendula Hand Balm to take home. I smiled as I put them into one of our cute recycled bags that we'd decorated ourselves with little rainbow stamps. Grace worked out her bill and she paid by cheque (we weren't set up for card payments by then) and then Saff helped her into her jacket.

We all said a cheerful goodbye and once she'd gone we looked at each other and...

"AAAAAAAAAAAAAAHHHHH!!!" we shrieked, so loud I'm surprised the glass shelves didn't shatter.

"She loved it, didn't she?" cried Grace.

"She went with the nail colour I suggested and said it looked really good," beamed Saff.

"She bought the last one of my hand balms too," I cried. "Summer's mum was right when she said they'd sell like hot cakes. I'll have to make a new batch."

"OMG, this is amazing!" squealed Saff. "I still can't believe we're really running this place!"

Then we got into a huddle and started leaping up and down, going whoo-hoo!

Mum raised her eyebrows. "We've been open a week now," she said. "Are you going to be like this after every single booking?" She was beaming too, though, and she let us pull her into our bouncy, dance-y hug.

We were still jumping around reception when the bell above the door jangled and Summer walked in, wearing a yellow-checked sundress and flip-flops. I'd missed her over the last few days. We'd only met a couple of months ago when I'd started at school down here, but already we were giggling our way through lessons together, and hanging out on the field with Marco and Ben at lunchtimes.

"Hi!" she said brightly.

"Hiya," I said, giving her a big hug.

Mum, Grace and Saff all said hi too and Mum asked how the camping had been. "Oh, you know, field, tent, torrential rain, the usual," said Summer cheerily. "You all look really happy. Is business booming, then?"

"Not too bad actually," said Mum. "We had lots of bookings right after our launch at the town fayre, but we do need to get some more in the diary for the next fortnight, especially during the week."

"Mum, seeing as that was your last client, do you think maybe Summer and I could have a treatment?"

"Go on then, you deserve it," said Mum.

"Thanks, Kim," said Summer.

"Not that you need a beauty treatment," I grumbled, as we went over to the chiller counter to pick out a fresh face mask each. Summer had peachy perfect skin, beautiful long eyelashes and thick glossy dark curls. She never bothered with make-up and only ever wore a slick of my orange-flavour lip balm on her pouty lips.

"Yeah, right, like you're not the Blonde Bombshell Babe of Year 9," she cried. "Well, Year 10 when we go back in September! The one who changed Marco from a super-player to Boyfriend Material."

I couldn't help grinning at that. The Marco bit, I mean. From the moment we met on my first day at school here in Totnes, when he pulled me out of the rain, there was this spark between us. And last Saturday, after the grand opening of Rainbow Beauty, I'd finally got to kiss him. But as for the rest of what she said…yeah right! At best I'm okay looking, if I wear loads of eye make-up. Otherwise, with my pale skin and lashes, and almost white-blonde hair, it honestly looks like I don't have a head. I told Summer that and she rolled her eyes. "Oh, Abs, don't start on with the headless thing again!" she groaned.

"I'm just saying, I need a bit more help than you in the beauty department," I insisted. "Especially as Marco's back tomorrow…"

Is romance in the air for Abbie…
or are there storm clouds up ahead?
To find out what happens next, read

ISBN: 9781409540557

eBooks also available

Which Rainbow Beauty girl are you?

Are you sassy like Saff, a great student like Grace, or simply adorable like Abbie? Take this fun quiz to discover which Rainbow Beauty sister you're most like!

1. Which flavour lip balm suits you best?
A) Peppermint; fresh and full of zing
B) Orange; warm and fruity
C) Strawberry; sweet and scrumptious

2. In ten years, you will be...
A) Doing some kind of sociable, creative job
B) A top businesswoman
C) Starring in your own TV show

3. What's your favourite subject at school?
A) Art – time to dream, draw and be creative
B) Maths – you love a bit of number-crunching!
C) Lunch – a perfect chance to catch up
 with friends over some tasty treats

4. Which word describes you best?
A) Positive
B) Sensible
C) Bubbly

5. School is for...
A) Seeing my friends, learning loads of cool stuff and having a good time
B) Studying and finding exciting new challenges
C) Showing off my new outfits

6. You've got £10 of your pocket money left to last you the week. Do you:
A) Spend it on supplies for making, baking, drawing, writing or designing
B) Save it – there's a new album you want coming out next month
C) Spend it on a new eyeliner – there's a dazzling smoky-eye effect you really want to try out!

Now turn over to discover your
Rainbow Beauty identity...

So which Rainbow Beauty sister are you?

Mostly As: Abbie

Just like Abbie, you always find the good in everything and your creative approach can help brighten any situation. You are a ray of sunshine to your friends. Just don't forget to treat *yourself* too – you deserve it!

Mostly Bs: Grace

Just like Grace, you're a straight-A student with the brain of a top businesswoman. You can be shy at times, but are a loyal and lovable friend once someone gets to know you. And when you put your mind to something, you're unstoppable...

Mostly Cs: Saff

Just like Saff, you've got bags of confidence and love being in the limelight. With hard work and dedication, you're destined for great things. Just remember that even budding celebs need to hand in their homework occasionally!

Super Smoothie Recipe!

Whizzing up a *Rainbow Beauty* fruit smoothie is a super-speedy and delicious way to help ensure you're eating plenty of fresh fruit. Eating healthily is brilliant for boosting your energy, while feeding your skin and hair with all the ingredients to give you a gorgeous glow.

Remember the Rainbow Beauty motto:
Beauty from the inside out!

Mum's Magnificent Mango Smoothie

You will need:
1 ripe mango
1/2 lime
150ml (1/4 pint) apple juice
2 tablespoons clear honey

If you don't have a jug-style blender or smoothie-maker, you can use a handheld blender instead.

1. Slice the mango lengthways, on both sides of the stone. If you haven't done this before, get someone

to help you. Peel off the skin. Then, cut the flesh away from the stone and put it all in a jug-style blender.

2. Squeeze out the juice from half a lime. Add the lime juice, apple juice and honey to the blender. Put on the lid and whizz everything together.

To make this an extra-special *Rainbow Beauty* smoothie, pour it into a tall glass and top with a slice of lime and a sparkly straw.
Invite your friends over for a smoothie date, put on a feel-good playlist and celebrate being YOU!

For more mouthwatering recipes that are perfect for parties, sleepovers and girly nights in, check out

ISBN: 9781409532767

What did you want to be when you were younger?

A story writer! I made a book of poems when I was about six and my dad block-printed the covers on an old mangle. Then I sold them to my friends and relatives — yes, for money! I was one cheeky kid!

What's the best piece of advice someone's ever given you?

Erm… Be yourself. That's good advice. And the best thing I've learnt myself is don't go over and over past mistakes — do what you can to put things right, learn from them and then look to the future! Oh, and never tie your shoelaces in a revolving door.

Which character do you most identify with?

I think writers put a little of themselves into lots of

their characters. I guess I most identify with Abbie, as I'm quite enthusiastic and passionate about stuff (and think too much about things!). I can also be like Marco, especially with his fear of rejection. Ben and Summer are the kind of easy-going, chilled people I love to have as friends in real life – I wish I could be more like them!

What is your favourite Rainbow Beauty product from the book?

The Rose and Geranium Bath Bombs. They sound so delicate and pretty. And nothing beats relaxing in the bath with your fave book and some chocolate.

Do you think you could run your own business?

Being an author *is* running your own business. As well as writing, you are your own marketing and PR person, receptionist and office manager, researcher, accountant, post room, and you even have to make the tea!

What's your most cringe-worthy moment?

OMG, there are so many! I'm like Abbie in that respect! One of the worst was when I was Abbie's age, waving to a boy I liked as I cycled past him and not looking where I was going. I smacked straight into a parked car, flew onto the boot and then had to get down and pretend to be fine!

We love Abbie's positivity. What makes you smile and keeps you positive?

My fab friends make me laugh. My amazing, funny children, Holly and Freddie, make me laugh. And my lovely husband, Matt, makes me laugh! I love funny stories and watching comedy on the TV and listening to it on the radio. And when all else fails, Curly Wurlys usually do the trick!

For all the latest news from Kelly,
check out

www.kellymckain.co.uk

Calling all Abbie fans!

For exclusive Rainbow Beauty material log on to

www.kellymckain.co.uk/rainbowbeauty

 Join in with all the latest *Rainbow Beauty* chat online

Be the first to know about *Rainbow Beauty* competitions and giveaways

Download gorgeous *Rainbow Beauty* screensavers and friendship vouchers

Learn how to do your own DIY manicure – perfect for that Saturday sleepover

Discover Kelly's fave pampering treats

And lots, lots more!

Thank you, thank you, thank you – MWAH!!!!

I had great fun making up all the lotions and potions for *Rainbow Beauty*, with the help of two great books, by beauty-product gurus Gill Farrer-Halls and Elaine Stavert.

I was hugely inspired by the fabulous Lush store in Covent Garden, where I spent MANY happy hours looking at (and testing out!) all the products (thanks, Raine – mwah!!). Of course, I had to buy and try lots of lovely things at home too (SUCH a hard job I have – hee hee!) and I even had a go at making some myself, and got loads of info from professional natural-product maker Andrea Shell to help me (cheers, babes!).

Totnes, where *Peppermint Kiss* is set, is a real (and super-fab) town in Devon, and lots of the locations in the book are really there, like the castle and Vire Island, although there's no actual *Rainbow Beauty* (aw, shame!). I first discovered it because my friend Jess grew up there – she was also one of the inspirations behind Lucy Jessica Hartley from the *Totally Lucy* books – thanks for lending me yet another bit of your life, Jess!

As you can tell I fell in love with the place. I have a map on my wall and pictures of key locations, and loads of notes about things like how long it takes to walk between places, and which supermarkets they have. Thanks go to John Giorgi from the Totnes Information Centre too, for all the extra help and info.

Huge thanks go to Matt, as ever, and to Ros, Nicky and Andrea for non-writing-related support in the form of curry nights, child entertainment and loads of laughs!

Thank you, thank you, thank you all – MWAH!!!

Kelly McKain
xxx

For more gorgeous, girly books
check out
www.usborne.com/fiction